P R I V A
P R O P E R T

PRIVATE PROPERTY

STORIES

DEBRA JO IMMERGUT

TURTLE BAY BOOKS

A DIVISION OF RANDOM HOUSE · NEW YORK · 1992

Copyright © 1992 by Debra Jo Immergut
All rights reserved under International and Pan-American Copyright
Conventions. Published in the United States by Turtle Bay Books, a
division of Random House, Inc., New York, and simultaneously in
Canada by Random House of Canada Limited, Toronto.

Portions of this work were originally published in *American Short
Fiction* and *Antietam Review*.

Gratitude is due to the editors of those publications and, for their
generous support, to James Michener and the Copernicus Society of
America. Heartfelt thanks also to Henry Dunow, Susan Kamil, and
especially, for everything, to John Marks.

Library of Congress Cataloging-in-Publication Data
Immergut, Debra Jo.
Private property : stories / Debra Jo Immergut.
P.   cm.
ISBN 0-394-58624-7
I. Title.
PS3559.M5P75   1992
813'.54—dc20   92-53662
Designed by Iris Weinstein
Manufactured in the United States of America
98765432
First Edition

FOR MY MOTHER AND FATHER,
AND SCOTT AND STEVEN

CONTENTS

RIVER ROAD 3

TENSION 23

FROZEN NIAGARA 41

LADY LIBERTY 59

LOTS 79

THE NUMBER
OF MY HEART 95

TRY HARD
TO BE GOOD 123

AVOIDING DARLA 137

PAYABLES 167

THE SKIRT 187

PRIVATE
PROPERTY

RIVER
ROAD

This life I am living now began last spring, a hot one, when we drove out River Road, the blossoms frying on the trees and my father just starting to dye his hair red. I was newly back in town then, and one bright Sunday morning in April, I'd glimpsed myself in the closet-door mirror: flattened across the mattress, arms dangling over the side, pulling apart dust balls.

So I decided to drive out to Potomac. It was something I'd promised myself I wouldn't do often. But I called my mother anyway. "I'm coming over," I said.

"Sweetheart. I'm showing a house today. I know, just terrible, every Sunday. This one's a biggie." Her voice brightened. "Your father, though—he'll be back from his game at noon."

Right then, right there, I saw the unexpected rising up. An afternoon together, Dad and his daughter. It had been a while. Steering my car up the garage ramp, over the last speed bump and tipping out into the daylight, I remembered: a spring day like this one, three years earlier, we'd rented a paddleboat on Assawaman Bay. My high school graduation was a month off. We pedaled way far out on the brackish water. We even sang, our old favorite: "I'll Never Fall in Love Again."

It was a few days later that the DrugTown people phoned him at home during the dinner hour, asking about the large quantity of Class 2 painkillers—Dilaudid, Percodan, Demerol—being prescribed in his name. "Out of the ordinary, we think, for your sort of practice," they said.

"Couldn't agree more," my father said. "May I ask who comes to claim it?" The person they described—ash-blond hair, red leather purse, silver rings on her right hand—was me. I was sitting right there at my pork chop, next to Mom, when Dad hung up the phone and turned toward me. "It's because I live with the unhappiest people on earth," I blurted out, then looked away from their shocked faces and whispered down at my plate: "Living here makes me mad."

Driving west on the parkway, the green frizz of spring trees whipping by, I recalled the aftermath of that evening. Over a painful summer I came and went, trudging through a household swamp of disappointment and shame, to meetings with a bored counselor or my state-assigned social worker, to group sessions at a local hospital, overwrought and exhausting. Hot months passed with averted glances between my father and me. He buried himself in sports-talk shows played loud on the living room radio.

Mom seemed defeated, and a little afraid of me. She'd tap at my bedroom door and ask from the hall if I needed anything. "I'm okay," I always said. In the middle of that July, she applied for her real estate license.

The next spring, with the chemicals' grip finally loosened, nineteen years old, I settled on acting and, ignoring all advice, picked up for New York, where I stayed for two years. My best part was as an oppressed female bakery worker who shits in the dough. My ex-boyfriend Duke played the bakery owner—that was how we met. Right before the spring I am telling of now, on Lincoln's Birthday, Duke left me for somebody whose star seemed to be rising on a steeper grade than mine. That precipitated my move south, back to what my mother calls "the home vicinity."

On that April Sunday, when I walked into the house, Cookie, the half-breed part Alsatian, yanked her head from the open trash compactor and wagged her tail. The back door was open. I heard someone guffaw and say, "Too good to be true, just too good." I walked out to the patio. My father was there with a man I'd never seen before.

"Hey, hey," my father said, seeing me in the doorway. He stood up and smiled, his cheeks round and reddened, as if from the sun on the golf course. "Hello my darling, hello, hello, what a delightful surprise."

When he jokes around or is drinking, he sometimes adopts a trilling, singsong voice, and spouts high-society talk, in the manner of some pearl-chokered lady in a Marx Brothers movie. He's dramatic, like me.

He walked over and put his arm around my shoulder, and squeezing it a bit, he said, "Meet my one and only daughter, Valerie, light of my life. Just moved back from New York City." The other man nodded; he looked a little older than my father, with rimless glasses and thin cheeks, and sand-colored hair slicked back from a high, bony forehead. Rising from his chair, he shook my hand and said, "Wyatt Moore, how do you do." I recall a yellow shirt and dark plaid trousers shot through with red. He was long-armed and skinny, but looked solid, not gangly, and the orange patio chair creaked as he sank back into it.

He picked up a near-empty glass, rattled the ice around, then tipped it to his mouth. Crunching, he said, "Well, isn't it great, now you live in town, you can drop by on a Sunday and have a day with your dad."

"You need a refill," my father said. "And you, my dear?" I said a drink would be fine, vodka tonic. He banged through the screen door, into the kitchen.

"You see my new car out there?" the man said.

"I don't think so." There was only my father's GTO in the driveway—a black convertible.

"I'm gonna buy that old Pontiac GTO," he said. "That's a classic muscle car."

I squinted at him. My father had bought that car with the first-year earnings from his practice, 1969. This

Wyatt sneezed, very loudly, then gazed at me and nodded. "That's how your father and I got to know each other, saw him getting into that Goat and I just had to pay my respects."

"He's selling the car?" I used to pull into the gas station, pom-pom girl peering out from the heart of that rumbling monster, and always some mechanic would ask me out.

My father pushed the door open, balancing three full highballs on a dinner plate.

"Jesus," I said, "it's a little hard for me to imagine you without that car. It's kind of your statement."

He set down the drinks on a pink metal table. "A minor adjustment. I thought I'd never get by without my '57 T-bird either."

"You had a Thunderbird?" Wyatt said. "I first touched tit in a Thunderbird. On New Year's Eve."

I smiled uncertainly, then glanced at my father, but he was gazing off into the woods beyond the backyard. "I believe I fondled my first breast in a movie palace," he said. "It was a nice breast, but not sizable." Then he turned back, and catching my eye, he shrugged.

I understood somehow that new ground rules were being laid then. New rules because I was paying my father a social visit, for the very first time. For the first time since I'd left home, I was just dropping in: no big crisis, no family holiday.

"Her name was Alice Peck. I think I was wishing for Mamie Van Doren," my father said.

A hot breeze slipped around the corner of the garage—and I thought the scene was strangely unfamiliar: sitting on the patio so early in the year, sipping vodka cocktails out of the wet glasses, sweating a little. Snow and ice had crusted over those flagstones just a month before. Now it was hot as summer, but too early for bugs: just the birds sang high in the trees.

"Robins everywhere out here," said Wyatt, "like pigeons." He drank, then swiped the glass across his forehead, leaving it shiny in the sunlight. He looked at me. "My wife and I live in the District," he said. "Behind the cathedral. Pigeon crap all over the place. What is it about cathedrals and pigeons, you know?"

"I think they like the sound of the bells," my father said. I sank a last sip. I was hungry, I hadn't eaten anything, but I'd begun to feel pretty fine. My mother's Mexican clay pots stood by in a row, filled with dirt, blank, awaiting pansies. A little way off, between two white oaks, hung the ratty hammock where I used to spend hushed hours tangling with my teenhood boyfriends long after the house's lights had gone out.

"Springtime," my father said, sighing. He stretched his legs out, crossing them at the ankles, resting his hands on his small paunch. He also wore plaid pants, sea-green, and his old brown kick-around shoes with buckles. " 'In just spring, when the world is mud-luscious, the gimp-footed balloon man whistles far and wee.' " He raised his eyebrows at me as if I should be impressed. I was. I hadn't thought he'd have a line of poetry on tap like that.

"Your dad," Wyatt said, throwing his head back, looking up at the sky. "Your dad. Valerie, your dad is the most cultured character I've met this side of a Bangkok whorehouse. I mean it." He grinned at my father. "George, you're okay, and your daughter here is one terrific-looking young lady, if you don't mind my saying."

"Couldn't agree more."

Wyatt set his empty glass on a table, stood with a little groan, and, looking from me to my father, said, "Now, I'd like to take that car out on a little test drive, and I'd like you two to join me. What do you say, a Sunday spin out River Road?"

My father raised his eyebrows. "I haven't been out that way in years, I don't know how long." He seemed recklessly agreeable. He certainly was in Wyatt's thrall. The thought crossed my mind: who is this man? But it passed just as fast. That afternoon, Wyatt's appeal felt very strong, but still hazy to outline, tough to explain.

"What do you think, Val?" my father said.

"Come on, it'll be a hoot," said Wyatt. "Hand over those keys."

The rag top was down, and we were shooting over Falls Road to River. "So how're you going to spend your days here in our city?" Wyatt called to me.

"She's an actress," my father said from the front passenger seat. I was in back, my hair whipping around, feeling wild happiness, because as a kid, riding in this

backseat had been the most joyful thing on earth. I remember bouncing along, seven years old, clutching a
perforated paper bag with a noisy baby duck inside.

"An actress. Hot damn, no kidding." Wyatt let out
a whistle. "Wowee. An actress. Hard way to make a
living, though, I'd imagine."

"No way to make a living," my father said. Wyatt
chortled. "Just kidding, honey," my father added, catching my glance in the sun-visor mirror.

"Actress," Wyatt said. "Jamie Lee Curtis. Have you
seen her in a movie, George? Now there's a piece of
work. Man oh man." His words blew back and swept
over me like breath.

He made the turn onto River Road barely slowing
down, the tires sending out a yelp—the sound of high
school. "Takes balls to drive this car, Wyatt. I don't
know if you got 'em," my father shouted as we swerved
into the passing lane and blew by a flower-delivery van.

"As my wife's great-aunt Doris used to say, George,
fuck thee." All three of us laughed at that, the sounds
stolen from our mouths by the wind.

River road starts in the District, sprawls to four lanes in
the suburbs, and then funnels down and keeps on going,
way out to the west edge of the county, through poky
towns, Amelia and Suttersville. It ends at a Civil War hot
spot called Smith's Ferry. A flatboat crosses to the Virginia side over the brown and foamy river, which up there
is narrower and edged by woods.

The road turns to gravel in its last mile. "End of the line," Wyatt said, pulling up alongside a two-story building with a cracked coat of brown paint and a raised front porch. One plate-glass window wore a stenciled DAIRY STORE; the other was lit up by neon beer signs. Wyatt hopped out of the car, pushed the driver's seat forward to let me out.

Just past the building, the road ended. A slab of buckled concrete that I guessed was the loading ramp sloped down through the mud and into the dark water. Parked nearby, a couple in a silver Town Car waited for the ferry to chug back from the far bank. Next to the ramp were a few wooden shotgun houses.

"Well, we're out here," I said. The alcohol and the wind and the country road had worn me down a bit, and I was queasy. Wyatt climbed the sagging porch steps, checking around. I leaned against the side of the car where my father sat looking in the visor mirror and running his fingers through his hair.

"The Goat's still got kick," he said, or something like that—I barely heard. I barely heard because I was staring at his hair. In the strong light flooding through the trees, pouring down on his head, I saw that his hair's normal color—grizzly brown scattered with gray—was changed, redder somehow. His curls looked rusted and stiff, like the bared innards of a mattress abandoned behind some motel.

"You're coloring your hair," I said. The sunlight, heavy and bright, was scorching the air, making it hard to breathe. My father's gray, more apparent each time I saw him, had been some proof that life moves in one direction and one direction only, despite my wavery vision of the world, my meanderings, my doubts.

" 'Auburn Lustre,' " he said. "Elise does it, at my barber's." His brows squeezed together, brows that didn't quite match his hair. "I hope you're not going to say I shouldn't."

"It's just unexpected. I'm not sure why you're doing it."

He peered into the mirror and said, "I want to look good. I don't want to get old, I guess."

"Fair enough." I felt dazed. "Are we taking the ferry?"

Wyatt walked down the steps, turned, and frowned in the direction of the barge, tied motionless on the far side of the water. "Nah," my father said. His forehead was wrinkled in a pattern of waving lines. "Hell, who wants to go to Virginia? Redneck state."

"You're talking about the state I live in now," I said.

"I suggest we refresh ourselves at the old saloon here," my father said.

"I wouldn't dream of spoiling the fun," Wyatt said, leading the way.

There was dust floating everywhere that afternoon. Gravel dust hung in a cloud above the parking lot a long while after our car pulled in. Gold powder shimmied through the air inside the bar, in the light streaming hot through the windows, a cyclone every time someone moved. It softened the red of the walls, the carpet, the shiny red booths. The scene glittered, as when snow falls on a theater stage. In my memory, the whole day looks that way.

Of course there was a jukebox playing, the sort that will make music whether somebody feeds it a coin or not. A few guys wearing white jerseys, 19, 17, 36, sat at the bar. Number 19—longish blond hair, small mustache—turned and watched the three of us coming in, not unfriendly, just looking. I was a little embarrassed, meeting his eye, realizing that I was out with two men in plaid golfing slacks.

Wyatt nodded to the man at the bar. "Hi there."

The man nodded back. "How're you today?"

"Never better," Wyatt said.

"Take a seat, what'll you have—Val?" my dad said, steering me over to a booth by the huge streaked window.

"Beer," I said, shaking his hand from my elbow.

"Hey, good idea, I'll have the same," Wyatt said, sliding in across from me. My father went up to the bar and stood next to 19. The bartender, an older woman with a blue rinse in her hair, wiped a rag down the bar toward where my father leaned against it, his foot on the metal rail below.

"So you live in Virginia. Whereabouts?" Wyatt asked me. He tapped the square top of his gold ring against the Formica table. His fingers were thin, knuckles sharp.

"Arlington. In an apartment complex."

"I get over there sometimes. I've got my little brother buried in Arlington. A lieutenant colonel in Vietnam, believe it or not. Crashed his car going home from watching the Super Bowl in '77." He looked at me and grinned. "He was a crazy stupid kid."

My eyes met his eyes. "So you met my father in a parking lot?"

"Nope. In his office. I sell pharmaceuticals."

"Really," I said. My hair, still tousled from the drive, was falling into my eyes, I guess. He reached over and brushed it back. I darted a glance at my father, turning from the bar, approaching with the beers. He hadn't seen.

He set three bottles on the table. "Slide over, hon," he said to me. "You and me drinking in the afternoon, your mother would be disgusted." He took a sip and shifted over to look at me. "That dress new?"

"Not terribly," I said. It was a rose-colored sundress, Indian cotton. It was the first time I'd bared my arms that year. They must have been pale and thin.

"It's pretty," he said.

The door to the bar opened and a woman in a pink sweater stepped in, followed by a man: the Town Car couple. "Any idea why the ferry's just sitting at the other side? There are people waiting out here," the man called, gesturing toward the parking lot, sunglasses in one hand.

The ballplayers stared over their shoulders. The lady bartender said, "Maybe the motor broke."

The man turned to his companion. She shrugged a

little and smiled. She rested a hand on her purse and passed her gaze around the bar, past us, past the guys at the bar and the woman pouring peanuts into blue plastic bowls, past the jukebox and the black tables and red swivel chairs and the tiny teak dance floor laid over a corner of the shag carpet.

The woman walked across the room. I noticed my father following every step of her black pumps, the graceful swish of white linen trousers. With her bright lipstick and sleek dark hair, she could have been a saleswoman of expensive cosmetics, or a designer of some kind. She'd certainly realized something; I'd felt it, too. This bar was the sort of place where you could disturb the energy patterns by moving your hips, your eyes, in a certain way.

She sat in a swivel chair and said, "I'd love a drink, anyhow."

The companion, boyfriend, husband, said, "Tanqueray and tonics over here, okay, miss?" to the bartender, and dragged a chair up close to the woman's.

My dad looked at Wyatt, and then at me. He laughed, stretched his arm above my shoulder along the back of the banquette, and said, "A Sunday adventure. That's what we're having!"

"What do you sell?" I said to Wyatt.

"Well. I don't sell anything at all, directly. My job is to get doctors like your father interested in our product, get them to prescribe it to their patients."

I looked at my dad, who was staring off past Wyatt's shoulder. His eyes flickered between a silent basketball game on a TV above the bar and the young woman at the table, who snapped open a compact, brushed a flake of mascara from her cheek.

"My sample case alone's got a street value of more than three hundred grand. Barbiturates, morphine derivatives, et cetera."

My father tuned in to the conversation then. He glanced at Wyatt, frowned, and then looked at me. I shrugged. "That's impressive," I said.

As the sun cut through the window in lower and lower angles, more and more golden, my father's dye job looked more and more fake—almost wiglike. It chilled me to see it. We'd switched back to vodka. Wyatt had gotten up to look at the jukebox selections, and the woman at the table was smoothing her hand along the arm of her man's striped sport shirt, tipping her head against his shoulder.

My father said, "Your mother doesn't fulfill me."

I sat up bolt straight. "Don't say that to me. Why would you say that to me?"

"Making love is not work. Making love is supposed to be something. . . ."

"Hey," I said, my throat tensing. "Hey. Hey."

He looked down at the table. His face became rumpled, distorted, as if by an awful, powerful G-force. I watched him, feeling sick, and a little panicky. An old Frank Sinatra song reared up from the jukebox, swinging horns and suggestive bass notes. Wyatt appeared by the booth and held out his hand. "Dance with an old man, Valerie?"

With his hand like a gun on the small of my back, Wyatt guided me to the patch of wood set aside for dancing. He held me six inches away from his body, scrupulously, one hand loosely holding mine, the other resting on the curve of my waist. My arms and legs felt as if they were wooden parts, hinged. My left hand lay lightly by the collar of his shirt. I looked up at him, moved my mouth in a sweet automatic smile, then looked at the insignia embroidered on his breast pocket the rest of the time we danced. It was a wreath of tiny green leaves. I went through that leafy circle, lay cradled there like a nymph in her bower.

Should my father have been more vigilant? You might say: of course. But he had his own pains in life, ripe disappointments that clung closely to him, wouldn't fall away.

Wyatt was singing along. "How long I wondered, could this thing last?" He dipped me a little. "But the age of miracles, it hadn't passed. . . ." I felt alone, I knew I was alone. Wyatt's hand was moving down my back and hip, pressing the thin material many times over. When he leaned and kissed my neck, I smiled up at him. I murmured, "That's nice."

Then, suddenly, I heard my father's voice across the room: "What the——" I pulled away, Wyatt jerked his head up. My father had tried to stand, but the booth's table hit the tops of his legs; he fell back into the seat. He sat there, for a moment, disbelieving.

I froze to the spot; then he was barreling across the room, his hand closing around my forearm. Gray in the face, muttering harsh undecipherable words, he hustled me out, out to the car. We left Wyatt standing there on the dance floor, arms folded across his chest.

When we finally got back to the house, the edges of the sky were dark. My father climbed out of the GTO, unlocked the front door, and disappeared inside without a word, but he left the door open behind him. I stood on the walk, trying to let the heat in my forehead and cheeks dissipate, trying to figure out what to say. In a minute I heard the clean whisper of the kitchen faucet running, and the small clinking of my father rinsing the glasses in the sink. The water stopped; then came the television, a sports announcer reading the scores of spring exhibition baseball games. I walked to my car, got in, and drove back to Arlington.

Wyatt has told me the story of his hitchhike home that Sunday many times, in my apartment late on midweek nights. Though he rations them carefully, there's always one or two of those physician's samples in the top drawer of the nightstand. When he launches into the story of that afternoon again—or almost any of his stories, I have to admit—I roll over, away from him, to slip down into that drawer and drift in my wide-eyed dreams.

I see us riding home, my father and me, him pushing

the GTO's engine all the way. Our sadness rides between us like a hot-breathed family hound. We roar, rag top down, past farms and subdivisions, Amelia and Suttersville, homes drenched in lowering light. We blast by with loose crazy winds fluttering around our necks, trailing behind us like scarves.

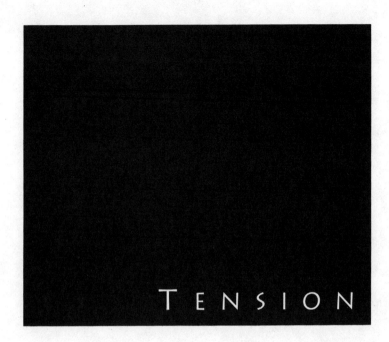

TENSION

Every summer when the kids go away to camp, Jolie expects something to happen. We'll fall in love all over again, or I'll suddenly develop an interest in the *Mystery Theater* she likes to watch on TV. She takes the bus home early from work to fix special dinners for me. I know she's hoping for romance when I see pointless frills of lettuce filling the empty space on the plates. I've seen such signs for four or five summers now. I suppose it's her response to the quiet that rolls into the house like a fog when our two kids finally hoist their bright duffels and go. To burn it off, that fog, she wants desire, our eyes locked in sizzling contact, sex in the living room. My hands on her body.

It was, incredibly, just about a week ago today that I stopped by Jolie's office unannounced in the midafternoon. I lobby for synthetic-textile producers—who weave not only panty hose but also the supersensitive tissue of missile-seeking satellites—and was hiking up from K Street for a hearing on the Hill. It was a relief to come indoors that day, though government buildings are kept only moderately cool, wet air blown around by weak fans. Jolie's cubbyhole at Health and Human Services is at the end of a hall on the ground floor, its one window opening onto the center of a dense holly bush.

"Surprise, surprise!" she said when I sidled in, banging her chair with the door. She swiveled in her seat and grabbed both my arms, pulling me into a metal chair jammed between the desk and the wall. "What could possibly bring you to my domain?" She smiled widely, tilted her head. She wears her honey-brown hair smoothed back from her forehead, the soft curved ends falling to brush against her earlobes.

"Stopped to tell you I'll be home late," I said, trying to wedge my briefcase into the space above my knees. "Don Nixon's got a ticket to the basketball game."

When I looked up, the smile had vanished from her face.

"I'm not sure who's playing," I said. "I think it's Bullets–Knicks."

"I've got veal medallions defrosting." Jolie looked at me with stricken brown eyes.

The kids had been gone a little over three weeks: Jolie's campaign of fussy dinners was in full swing. I'd watch as she'd regale me with salmon steaks and gossipy, amusing stories, beam at me across an elaborate dessert,

some peach roll-up or a fattening parfait. What arose in
me was nothing like desire. It was, instead, a strange,
stolid sort of angst, which I'd disguise by leafing zombie-
like through trade journals or scouting down the *Newsweek*
that came in the mail. "How about a little Drambuie,
Martin?" she'd try. "Thanks but no thanks," I'd refuse.
Eventually, drawn by the din of our furiously mowing
Canadian neighbors, she'd wander to the picture window
and murmur that perhaps she'd tackle some lawn work.
And soon, a sight to fill me with contrition: my wife, on
hands and knees, weeding the beetle-ravaged rose bed, or
cantilevered over the steering wheel of the old red Toro,
buzzing speedily back and forth in the blue evening outside the window. Jolie behind the wheel makes me think
of high school, years and years ago, when the lawmen in
our Ohio town knew her yellow Cougar well. With her
sweet shyness and her quick, rather devastating smile, she
charmed her way out of a small fortune's worth of cita-
tions.

On this particular afternoon I felt a strong impulse to
steer clear of the dinner scenario. "What's so bad?" I
said, standing up. "It's a basketball game."

She clicked a ballpoint in and out. "Fine."

"All right." I turned back to look at her, hit my knee
against the door frame. I looked down upon her bowed
head, her round shoulders with the bra straps showing
through her white summer blouse.

"You've been being impossible."

I said, "I'm being as cooperative as I can."

"It's such an effort for you." She stared down at her fingers, the pen.

"Jolie," I said. I bent over, took one of her hands, lightly tanned, and squeezed it. She raised her face and stared at me with a sadness that straightened me up, away from her. "I won't be home late, promise," I said, giving her hand an extra pressure before releasing it. She nodded. She looked skinny in her cheeks, drawn. I walked back out along the buffed linoleum hallways. The halls of government I've walked, if laid end to end, would take me far away. Caracas, Venezuela, or an island in the Arctic Ocean.

Last summer Jolie thought I was screwing around. She was wrong—but not all wrong. (About my true lapse, four and five years ago, she never suspected a thing.) During the sticky June of last summer I had, in fact, fallen in love. Someone at work, a junior partner aged thirty, hired away from a public relations outfit in New York. Through the depths of midsummer, I couldn't bring myself to go to bed when Jolie did. I'd lie instead on an afghan spread in front of the den's air-conditioning unit, holding a beer on my chest, listening to the sounds from the bedroom—hangers rattling as Jolie hung up her robe, sink on and running, then off, the alarm blaring momentarily as she set it. Visions of my workplace love would flutter across my mind. Her long fingernails, flicking open the brass catches of her briefcase. The sweep of her cheekbones, her teeth when she laughed, her dark curly lashes, sheened eyelids lowering. The different outfits she wore—I'd begun to notice the patterns there. She often appeared on Fridays in a sky-colored suit with an ivory silk blouse. It was on one such Friday I finally asked her to have a drink with me. At the bar, she said, "May I be indiscreet with you?" and as my pulse clattered she pushed aside the drink I'd ordered for her and leaned forward, her lovely manicured hands flat on the tabletop. "This is top secret," she said, flashing a grin. "I'm four months pregnant and I can't believe how happy I am. I feel like the only thing left for me to wish is to have twins—because I don't know if one baby's going to be enough for how much love I feel."

"Children *are* awe-inspiring," I said. "Absolutely."

By the time Andrea and Kenny returned from Camp Piney Rock that August, my fascination had died down to a flicker now and then, when I heard her sweet voice— "Four copies of that, okay?"—in the corridor outside my office.

Jolie, though, was convinced I'd been unfaithful in more than a mental way. Once, as I was stretched out on the afghan with my beer, she curled down onto the floor next to me, pressed her face to my chest. Her breath passed warmly through the weave of my undershirt. "What's wrong?" I said. She shook her head. After a while, she was asleep, sad and soundless as a spirit.

The Bullets play at an arena in Landover. We battled traffic the entire way. Nixon drove, and I watched the sun set above the Beltway as a thousand taillights burned, like embers.

The game was sluggish, low-scoring, not worth recounting. Darkness and stillness had flattened the neighborhood by the time I got home. I tried to be extremely quiet as I entered the house through the side door: if Jolie was asleep, I didn't want to wake her.

From the kitchen, I glimpsed her in the living room, watching the late news. Her hair was all in clips, tight against her head, and her face was a still moon in the light from the television. I called hello to her and stopped to investigate the refrigerator. She said something I couldn't hear.

"What?" I said, walking to the doorway with a plum in my hand.

"This time I want to know," she said, not turning from the screen.

I stood still under the door frame, the plum cold and soft against my palm. "Know what?"

"Please don't mollify me," she said. I'd never heard her use that word before. "You've got nothing for me. I see that." She pulled a throw pillow out from behind her and placed it on her lap. "Everything's a chore." She smoothed her fingers around the pillow's piped edges. I watched her from the doorway, knowing I should go to her, but suddenly cemented to the spot where I stood.

Pushing herself up, Jolie approached me, her bare feet making light sticking noises on the floorboards. "Martin, please tell me something truthful—anything."

"Don't be ridiculous," I blurted. My nerve endings were dancing. A wild energy surged through my shoulders, my neck. She stepped in front of me, face turned up. A few thin hairs, sprung loose from their restraints, tickled the shiny surface of her forehead. She said, "So why don't you tell me who you're screwing?"

"Jolie." My voice shocked me; it sounded strained. I dropped the plum. It landed with a tiny smack and rolled by her foot. She didn't seem to notice.

"Is it the hot weather?" she said.

"No," I said.

"Or am I driving you away?"

It happened then—my arm flew back and my fist slammed into her face.

She fell backward; the back of her head thumped on a bookcase. Her eyes closed as she landed on the floor, then opened wide, staring at me, dull and uncomprehending, reflecting the television light.

"Oh Jesus," I yelled. My fist was throbbing. "Jolie, Jolie, are you all right?"

She lay there, staring. I kneeled down to her. She covered her nose with one stiff hand and started to cry. She squeezed her lids shut, tears swelled from beneath them, and black blood started to rush from her nose. It dripped over her lips and chin and soaked into the high collar of her nightgown.

I tried to take her hand away from her face. "Let me look."

She rolled to face the wall. "Get away," she whispered. She curled her body around a large potted plant.

I dashed to the kitchen, scrambling for a dish towel, my mind roaring, a thought crashing repeatedly in my inner ear: "I love her, I love her, I love her." In eighteen years, I'd never before come close to hitting my wife. I banged my head on an open cabinet door. Stumbling back to the living room, I held the towel up to my forehead in pain. My wife, Jolie, was lying there, snuffling her own blood. I stooped over her, panting. As I mopped her face, I sobbed, "Sorry, I'm sorry." She moaned muffled phrases into the towel, turning her face away from me. I still don't know what she was saying then. I could not hear a thing—only a thrumming across my eardrums, a world-drowning sound, a terrible rumbling of love and shame.

In the emergency room, a bone-thin elderly black woman in an old-fashioned starched white cap took one look at Jolie in her robe, with the homey checked towel soaked reddish-brown on her face, and fixed me with a glare. I wanted to protest, to explain—but I was cowed by her righteousness. I signed the admission forms and avoided the old lady's eyes, skulking around the waiting room. At last, an impassive young resident called me into a small examination room, where the stiffening dishrag accused from a plastic waste bucket near the door. Jolie was nowhere to be seen.

Broken nose, he said. Necessitates an overnight stay, perhaps more. Damage to this and that area, may have to be rebroken before setting. Please see nurse for the appropriate forms.

After a night passed lying atop the bedcovers, tossing through dreams of airplane plummets, I returned to the hospital. Jolie had asked the nurses to bar me from her room, and they carried out her orders with relish, with glee. I loitered in the deserted vending-machine lounge for an hour, feeling subhuman. During a changing of the guard, I made a run for it.

"Yes, angel," Jolie was saying into the phone. "I'm going to be fine." She looked at me, big eyes steady over the pure white bandages obliterating the middle of her round face. "Dad's not here right now, but I'll give him your love . . . Uh-huh . . . Okay, bye now."

I grabbed the receiver as she reached to hang it up. I pressed it to my ear. "Andrea honey?" The line buzzed back at me. I replaced it onto the cradle. "What'd you do that for?"

She shrugged.

"You told her what happened?" I said.

"No." She lightly tossed away the bed sheet to reveal green drawstring pants and a top. "They said I should walk this morning for a bit. Come with me?"

I grasped the offered hand to pull her up. "I would love to." I hooked my arm around her waist. She looked up at me, pinning me with those eyes. Her hair was sticking out at odd angles—odd but familiar angles, angles I'd seen every waking morning of our lives. I lifted my hand to smooth them out. Jolie batted it away, saying,

"I think my slippers are under the bed." I bent down to get them, little paper-and-cardboard things, demurely resting side by side in the spotless shadows beneath the bed.

Standing, I clutched the slippers to my chest a moment. "I'm miserable about this," I said.

"I know," Jolie said. She took the slippers from me and dropped them onto the floor, where they landed upright, one in front of each foot. She stepped into them.

And then there I was, walking the hospital grounds with my battered wife. Over her green uniform, she'd donned a silky robe I'd bought her that morning from an RN who sold lingerie out of a gym bag stashed behind the nurses' station. The pink fabric bloomed out behind her in the summer breeze. This was very nice weather for July in our city. Across from the hospital, three children wobbled on skateboards. They stared at us, these kids, as did their parents, unloading groceries from their car trunk. Jolie paraded by their stares, seemingly oblivious—Jolie, who'd never been showy for a moment, who always wore a cover-up at the beach.

"They will have to rebreak it," she said.

"Oh, they will," I said, nodding. Another sandbag of despair settled inside me, lodging itself heavily behind my ribs.

A man watering his begonias with graceful waves of a garden hose looked over his shoulder at us. Jolie gazed back at him dreamily. "Are you going to trim the back hedge?"

"Of course," I said, taking her hand. From a fenced-in side yard, a boxer railed at us.

Jolie stopped, pulled her fingers from mine, faced me. "I want you to move out."

"Jolie, please. Please. I don't know what happened to me last night, but it was a moment utterly disconnected from the rest of our marriage. You know that, you must."

"I don't know that. I don't think I can simply forgive you." She walked away from me a few steps, to a parked car, then turned and leaned against its hood. She sighed. "I'm tired of everything." It occurred to me that, reclining against the car's silvery surface, with her face half-hidden, with her billowy clothes and velvet slippers, she looked not a little like a harem treasure, the exotic dalliance of a sultan.

I must have been staring oddly; she scowled at me. "And you're also tired, I guess. It's like trying to get water from a rock with you," she said.

I ran a hand through my hair. "I love you, sweetheart. How can I tell you? None of your suspicions have been valid in the least." This was more or less the truth. I stepped up to her and took her gently in my arms. I kissed her hair. "We have two kids who need us."

She extricated herself. "I'll give it some thought."

"Yes, definitely, take your time," I said. She raised her face to look at me a moment, squinting her eyes. I tried to appear encouraging, supportive. Then she turned and began walking back toward the hospital. It loomed above her, its mirrored towers bouncing light back into the sky.

In the dead of night the phone rang. It was Jolie. "I'll stay with you," she said, "if you agree to this: you pay for and nurse me through a complete overhaul. By that I mean as long as I'm going under the knife anyhow, I'd like my eyes and chin done, my breasts lifted, and a tummy tuck."

"Your breasts lifted? What?"

"Is it a deal? Otherwise I'm filing for divorce, I'll call my brother's law firm tomorrow."

"You can't be serious here, can you?" I sat up and turned on the reading lamp. On the night table stood our wedding portrait in a scrolled frame. That endless day, she'd been truly, truly beautiful, holding my hand under the banquet table, dancing a cha-cha with my father; she'd been mesmerizing, her eyes dark with joy.

But she's lovely still, I thought, surely. "Where is all this coming from? You think this is what I want?"

"This is what *I* want. These are my terms. So tell me, do you accept them or don't you." Her voice was low and edgy, but determined.

I blew out a long breath. "I suppose it's out of this world, moneywise?"

"You bet."

I pressed my head back into the pillow and stared in silence at the ceiling for a moment. Then I said, "Sweetheart, for you, anything. I've always said it and I always will. To show you how much I love you."

"Good then," she said. The line clicked and she was gone.

Jolie cried out from our bedroom last night. "Stop him," she wailed, slurring her words. "He isn't correct!" I ran in from Andrea's room, where I'd been laying sleepless, and stroked her shoulder softly, telling her everything's all right, she's only having a Nembutal dream. I changed the bandages on her face again and, oh God, did she look horrible under there. As if a truck had hit her head-on. The staples in her skull were just starting to crust over a bit, which Roth, her doctor, said to expect.

Ultimately, Jolie decided against the tummy tuck, which would have necessitated a prolonged hospital stay. "Say so long to your wifey," she said with disturbing gusto as they settled her onto the gurney. "Make way for the new me."

Then the orderly trundled her off down the long stark hallway, and I heard myself whimpering.

Roth performed the procedure and afterward signed Jolie's release forms straightaway. He himself wheeled her out of the recovery room. I do not exaggerate when I say it was the worst fright of my life, seeing Jolie that way.

She was swathed almost completely from brows to breasts in bandages, some of which were faintly tinted with pink or yellow seeping up from underneath. The metal staples, five of them about an inch long apiece, glittered dully like jewelry across the brink of her forehead, and above them her hair, caked with blood and who-knows-what, poked up, darker at the roots. Her head lolled to one side, resting against the vinyl back of the chair. The gap marking her mouth glistened with saliva. She was moaning, a low bleating, hardly audible.

"Jesus," I said; I couldn't move toward her. "What happened? Is she okay?"

"Absolutely, everything's absolutely on target," Roth said. "She's in a tad of pain but otherwise just fine."

"This is fine? Looking like a car-bomb victim?" I took a step in their direction, but I still wouldn't get too close: what if I were to jostle her? She'd come apart in gelatinous pieces.

"Well, Martin, breaking someone's bones, flaying the skin from her body, scraping away nodes of tissue . . ." Roth looked at me, brows up, and shrugged. "It's not like getting your teeth cleaned."

A radio trilled classical music in the waiting room behind me. My wife slumped, ravaged, in the wheelchair. This is what it would be like if she were dead, I thought. There appeared to be so little left of her—she might die any minute now. A life empty of her unfurled before my eyes. No Jolie in the house, no house, no place at all.

Roth wheeled her around and pushed the chair's handles toward me. "She needs rest, and someone to change her gauze, and plenty of quiet. Now the nurse will show

you how to take care of her.'' He extended a hand for me
to shake. His eyes appeared dusted over, simply unin-
volved.

So now I'm caring for Jolie. I'm taking the entire week
off work. The neighborhood's more peaceful during the
day, and I've been trying to enjoy that. Yesterday,
though, after I finally got her safely home and into the
bed, I felt miserable. My limbs were limp from the
remorse. And I was racked with terrible visions of something going wrong with Jolie's healing.

Then, about an hour ago, she vomited. Changing the
pillowcases, mopping up the mess, I recalled how Andrea
and Kenny, until they crossed the threshold of ten years
old, invariably became carsick on family trips. And they
were never in sync—first one would go, and we'd clean
up, then the other would let loose. We walked all over
a freezing Boston once, looking for a replacement pair of
lacy girls' tights, and while doing that, we'd seen one man
throw another through a plate-glass window. We hurried
away with the kids—there was blood everywhere—but
the event left a mysteriously deep impression on me, and
the image of a man flying through Filene's window, the
huge sound of it, flashes before me at the oddest times.
I still wonder what they were fighting about.

After I finished cleaning up Jolie, swabbing her gently
with a dampened washcloth, I ran a warm bath and
stripped off my clothes. Usually, I enjoy short, hot show-
ers; it had been some time since I'd afforded myself the

luxury of a nice long soak. I even dropped in a handful of Jolie's bath bubbles. Easing into the water, I was unable to stifle a groan of pleasure at its sleek warmth slipping over my skin. I leaned back and closed my eyes. Then I opened them, reached for one of the magazines Jolie has stacked up in there. Some of the women in those fashion magazines are really put together well. Striking, in a wonderfully fresh way.

As a matter of fact, I tossed aside the magazine and climbed out of the tub. I walked, dripping, naked, to the bedroom. Standing over Jolie, I peeled the wet pads from her face. I forced myself to look, truly look for the first time at the mangled remnants of the face I've known best. I studied the blackened stitches, the seething golden welts, the enraged magenta of her taut closed lids. The wine-colored swellings over her cheekbones, her bruised lips. I even—I'll admit it—slid back the sheet and crouched down to get a side view of her new bust line.

I straightened up and gazed at her. I thought: Yes. Yes, okay. And something rolled up through me then, an anticipation, something wholly rejuvenating. It surged high inside of me, washing warmly through my welcoming soul.

So now I have drained the water from the tub. I've dried myself and dressed. A summer wind is up, and from where I stand by our bedroom window, our yard looks like a heaven on earth. The grass is shivery with light. I'm even looking forward with silly pleasure to trimming that hedge today, if I can locate the lopping shears.

FROZEN NIAGARA

Anthony's girlfriend announced it to everyone at the table: "He's lying." Touching her spoon to her nose, she tilted her head and smiled across the room at him. "You know you are. There weren't any clever stunts. No box of shoes." She looked around at their guests. Forking up chicken or the soft insides of baked potatoes, they flickered their gaze toward Anthony. "He got the job through connections," she said.

Anthony chuckled; he shrugged his shoulders and reached for the wine jug. His face, reddening, could have heated the room.

Then the petite girl seated next to him piped up: "I got a stereo-sales job once by wearing a padded bra." Everybody's attention shifted away from Anthony then, easy as that. He rose from the table and disappeared down the hall.

His girlfriend must have thought that, sleeping in his
bed, she had a right to reveal him. But I was his sister, and
I knew better. Anthony's untruths were more dear to him
than anything. Certainly more than that girl's black
leather skirt (though you might have been fooled, the way
he ogled her).

I could have been invisible at that party: I don't think
a soul noticed when I excused myself and headed down
the hall. I found Anthony rummaging through the pockets
of overcoats on the bed. He discovered car keys in a
parka.

"She's got a navy Le Baron, very nice," he said, then
looked up. "Time for me to go." He swung past me,
through the hallway to the front door.

There was no time to scout around for my coat—so
I snatched somebody's red plaid scarf and scurried after
Anthony into the cold night air. He was striding past the
row of cars parked along the deserted street, bouncing his
fist off each frost-covered hood.

"Anthony," I said, shivering, binding the scarf
around my hands.

He stopped at a Chrysler. I didn't know the car—I
hadn't known anyone at the party. They were friends of
Anthony's and the girlfriend's, from their office. Anthony
had told them this story—*story*—about sending the boss
some old wing tips and ladies' pumps, a joke about
"getting a foot in the door." It didn't sound like something he'd do, but who knows? The office people were
helping to break in the new place; Anthony and the

girlfriend had just recently moved in together, into the garden-apartment rental.

He unlocked the car and thrust himself in. "Anthony," I said, knocking on the passenger-side window with my muffled fists. He leaned over and snapped the lock open.

The seat wasn't cold, because it was plush velour, but the air in there was like a meat locker, like a morgue. Anthony turned to me. "I got the job by buzzing the office in a space shuttle."

"There's an idea," I said. He pressed his lips together, started the car, and maneuvered it through the byways of the apartment complex into the traffic on Rockville Pike. I tried to guess where he might be heading, tried to imagine his plan. We cruised past our childhood hangout, Pike Shopping Plaza, newly rustic with cedar shingles and wooden signs. Just beyond it, at a bus-stop shelter, Anthony braked and said, "I'm dropping you off."

"What—" I put my hand on the cool sleeve of his jacket. But I took it off right away—such a gesture was so unfamiliar. I think it frightened us both. But I couldn't get out. I climbed over the seat back instead, something I hadn't done in years—first one hammy thigh over, then the other. In the back, I curled up against the cold air, saying, "I'm going to sleep."

You love your brother no matter what, right? That's what I think. When we were little, he battered me daily or he

ignored me, absorbed in drawing his doomsday comics
and playing games in which tiny GIs attacked life-size fake
fruit. Anthony had long blond hair, knock-knees, and pale
blue eyes. He was shy around boys his own age, and the
kids on our block picked on him. He got into fights on the
way home from school. If I ran to get my mother to save
him, later Anthony would shove me and say I was a rat.
I was always worrying about him—he was forever getting
bloody noses—and I was always brokenhearted over
some name he'd called me, making fun of my freckles or
my crooked baby teeth.

In the chilly backseat, I lay hugging myself amid somebody's Styrofoam cups and scraps of paper. As I looked
up at the window from that strange angle, streetlights
blazed across my sight, along with signs, traffic lights
sometimes, a hash of dark branches against the sky. Anthony simply drove us. Soon I could tell we were whirling
down onto the interstate. I hung on tight.

I knew our direction was west from a sign that flew
by, upside down to my eyes. He switched on the radio
and tuned in a call-in show. "Where do folks eat more
French fries, in France or Belgium?" the host asked. A
lady got the right answer—in Belgium. I'd silently
guessed France—but when I heard the answer, I thought,
well, it never works to be tricky by being obvious.

Anthony sometimes let out a low, derogatory snort—
"Good guess, jerk"—when one of the contestants gave
an especially stupid answer, and once in a while he'd

twitch his head and utter a soft, distracted curse. But for the largest part he remained silent and it seemed, at times, as if he weren't there at all, as if I were drifting up into the west Maryland mountains in a ghost ship, or on a cloud, listening to the static raining down from outer space, laced with the tiny, excited voices from all over darkened America. That Chrysler gave a smooth, smooth ride. I began falling down into short spells of sleep and then bouncing back up from them, like someone jumping high and slow on a trampoline.

What made me think of it? Maybe someplace a billboard flapped past: SEE LURAY CAVERNS—THE SPLENDOR OF NATURE. I remembered Anthony's shrieks, echoing through the caves, bouncing off the seeping rock faces splashed with colored lights—purple and yellow, blue and green. Huddled beside my mother in the midst of the tour group, I knew he'd gotten into trouble again. Lagging behind, Anthony had tested, caressed, the slick, pearly tresses of a rock called Frozen Niagara. "Hands off, son!" a guard yelled, his voice reverberating through the darkness—drowning out in midsentence the guide lady's description of the Grieving Madonna.

Dad, when he finds him, belts him, hard. Anthony is now twelve and a half, constantly being reprimanded. He's got an "attention" problem, his teachers say, and a "truthfulness" problem. His cry wings through the caverns and soars up the ragged cathedral heights, a spectacular wail of distress. My father drags Anthony backward

along the neat paved trail, back to the earth's surface, to
the camper-choked parking lot, past families of tourists,
who gape. My mother and I stay below, stick with the
tour. Her face is tired. As we cluster obediently around
the Petrified Fried Eggs, she leans over and whispers, "I
made all my mistakes on Anthony. I'm correcting them
on you."

We stopped for gas at a Phillips 66 station. As we pulled
up to the pumps, I glimpsed the bright round sign over-
head, hung among the stars like a red giant—those stars
that are about to implode, and end up as either dwarves
or black holes, one of the two. While Anthony bent over
the gas nozzle, I stuck my head up carefully and looked
out—but it could have been a gas station anyplace on
earth. Across the road were dark woods and a wooden
house with Christmas lights sprinkled in the shrubs. Electric candle flames wobbled in the windows.

   The station's bright lamps revealed a brown cardigan
lying on the floor of the car, and I pulled it over me,
draping it around my face. The weave was loose enough
to see through. I watched as Anthony hurried by the
window and slid into the car. The engine started and the
white lamplight slipped away. After a minute or so, he
looked back at me. "You're not asleep." I pretended I
was. He turned back and settled again into a lounge-
driving position. "Well, free gas," he crowed. "Free
gas."

   Now we were really on the lam. I buried my fists in

the rough wool. The sweater smelled of cigarettes and one of the more popular perfumes. The police would be called. I thought about the partygoer who was missing the car. How long had it taken the people at the party to notice we'd gone? I pictured them standing on the thick yellow carpeting the live-in love had chosen, debating about what to do, one or two people around the fringes still sipping wine. But that scene would be hours over by now—she would be alone now, I guessed, hugging a sofa pillow, gazing miserably at the coffee table, at the broken-off chips in the dip and the bristling ashtray. Or maybe she waited in their bed, dozing with her face toward the door.

I mumbled, as if I were talking in my sleep, ''I question your taste in women.''

Anthony switched off the radio. ''I told her last week I wanted to move out. I'm through with her.''

That was a lie, I was absolutely certain.

I was nine, Anthony fourteen, when our father, driving drunk, killed a high school girl. His sentence was suspended, and a few mornings later, instead of going to work, he drove to Oregon. My mother began to cook for us, endlessly.

One evening not long after Dad's departure, I'm summoning Anthony to dinner, pushing open the door to his bedroom: he's wearing headphones. In a loud, rasping whisper and terribly off-key, he's singing, with his eyes squeezed shut and one hand holding up an invisible micro-

phone. He prances around the center of the room, teth-
ered to the record player. His knees flex, his hips swing
in a steady, gorgeous rhythm. Blue corduroys, swaying
arms. It amazes me; I've never seen this before, the grace
of a boy dancing. He doesn't know I'm there. Breathily,
he chants the heavy-metal words, a rhyme about wild
girls.

Then he opens his eyes. His audience of thousands
evaporates—it's just me, his chubby sister, standing
transfixed with one hand gripping the door frame. He
throws off the headphones. Music spills out onto the
floor, far-off, silly-sounding. "What?" he screams, tears
brightening his blue eyes. He lunges, pushes me down.
He grinds my face into the rug, his hand hot and tight
around the back of my neck. I'm choking out a desperate
giggle, but I want to tell him it's all right, I understand.
I really do believe he could be a star.

That night, his light is on late. I tap on the door and
go in. He is propped up in bed, bare-chested. By the light
of the reading lamp, I see sparse hairs on his chest, gold.
I perch on the edge of his bed, pulling the tattered hem
of my peach nightshirt over my round knees. The book
resting in his lap is *Out of the Silent Planet*. "You're
supposed to be asleep," he says.

"Teach me to kiss," I say.

He explodes with a short, disbelieving laugh.
"Maybe!" With his blanketed legs he kicks me off the
bed.

.   .   .

About an hour after we stole the gas, I heard Anthony's breathing change. We were driving very fast on some small road. I realized he was crying.

Anthony was my older brother. I never called him my big brother. But older. Your older brother is supposed to be your protector, someone to look up to. But now I was feeling his tears trickling inside me, burning hot.

"Please," I said. I sat up and rested my chin atop the backrest. It was twenty minutes past three, by the clock on the dash. "Why don't we pull over."

Anthony's wet face shone in the passing road lights. His eyes were mere slits, leaking tears. Certainly it was dangerous to drive like that. "We can stop for a second, can't we?" I pleaded. "Or are we late to get some-where?"

Ahead was a roadside fruit stand, boarded up. Anthony steered into the lot in front. The shuttered shack had an inward-turning look to it, as if it weren't just closed for winter but also needed time off to rethink. I leaned back against the seat and looked out at some bushel baskets upended in the snow, waiting for him to collect himself. Finally he blew out a long shaky breath, stretched his arms out in front of him, and clasped them behind his head. "Look," he said, "you've got to leave me alone."

"Why?"

"Put some thought into it." His voice sounded clogged and angry. "Think about it. If you love someone, does that make them always right?" Abruptly, he turned to look at me. "Answer," he said.

I shook my head. "I don't know." His aggravation shamed me. I hugged my arms close and stared out the window. Whether he was right or not? This had never seemed important to me.

"I'm not anybody so remarkable," he said.

I met his eyes. They were clear and intent, which surprised me. "Okay," I said. "Okay. You want to go home?"

"I do," he said, twisting back down to throw the car into gear. "That's exactly what I want."

In his second year of high school, Anthony started telling people that our father lived in California and was making his mark in television. This wasn't true. In his life with us, our father had worked for an advertising firm. He'd turn the television on at some time like 6:47 P.M. and silence us, and when the ad ended, he'd murmur proudly, "Superb."

What did he really do after he left us? At that point, we hadn't the slightest idea. Checks came monthly, but he didn't call, didn't write, and it wasn't until three or so years later, when Anthony was in serious trouble and Mom had to track Dad down to help with the hospital bills, that we found out. He was living in Portland with a Japanese woman named Micki, and together they'd opened a tavern called Don's. Why "Don's" we've never known—his name is Dan.

One day I was lounging in the kitchen after school, picking at my mother's coffee cake, and I heard Anthony and his friend Keith outside, Keith quizzing Anthony about our father in Hollywood. Anthony answers matter-of-factly—he has a big house by the ocean, sure, with a private movie theater—as they shuffle around beneath the basketball hoop. I decide I should do my homework outside in a lawn chair. Carrying my books out into the heat, I dawdle by the driveway in my dusty culottes and watch Anthony try to make a free throw. Keith, a boy whose ears look like round cookies poking through his long hair, says, "So can your dad get me Gloria Bunker's autograph?"

"Why should he?" Anthony says. He dribbles the ball once, then glances sidelong at me. On his sweaty T-shirt, a dark fan shape spreads between his shoulder blades.

"Our dad could get you her autograph, sure," I call to Keith.

"Shut up," Anthony barks. "Shut up!" He makes a quick move toward me then, and I squeeze my eyes shut. The ball slams into the garage door above my head.

I woke up to morning whiteness, silence—and I sat up.

We were parked on the side of a road. In front of the car a snowy hill loomed, with dark bluish fir trees climbing up the slope. Anthony was slumped against the door, one arm draped over the back of the seat, one over the top curve of the steering wheel.

His skin looked gray, and creased around the eyes. His yellow hair was dull and ruffled. He gazed at me, slack-faced—as he would have looked at a stranger on a bus or a subway. But then he said, "You remember burning your hand grabbing Mom's curling iron?"

"No."

"We were staying in a summer cabin at Hollow Lake."

He gestured past me with his chin. I looked over my shoulder. We were parked just on the far side of a bridge with pale green guardrails. Beneath the span, and far off on either side of it, a lake stretched as frozen and gray as if it were paved. It was set like a floor in the bottom of a narrow, pine-darkened valley, under heavy clouds.

"Oh, Jesus," Anthony groaned wearily, rubbing the heels of his hands over his face.

"I thought we were going home," I said. I curled my feet up onto the seat and wrapped my arms around my knees.

He twisted the rearview mirror and zeroed in close to it, studying himself, scratching the bristles on his chin. "Well, next best thing to home. Haneysville, Maryland."

"I guess." I yawned and rested my forehead on the cold window glass. I assumed we were wanted, on some kind of wanted list.

Two large brown birds were pecking around in the snow across the road. They weren't crows, and they weren't sparrows. They had bright blue feet and beaks.

"Know what?" I said. "There's no such thing as an untruth. If you think about it."

He looked down at the car floor, didn't reply.

"Know what I mean?" I said.

"Maybe," he whispered. He straightened the mirror, then moved his hand to the ignition.

"Wait," I blurted out. I didn't care to end it, suddenly, this time in nowhere. It felt to me like real togetherness. It reminded me of closeness. "Let me look around a little. I don't remember this place at all."

Opening the door, I uncurled myself from the seat. The air outside was cold and damp. I pushed the car door closed and with gingerly footsteps eased down the steep shoulder of the road, to a path of trampled, dirty snow leading to the base of the bridge supports. The trail might have been made by teenagers or ice fishermen, if there was such a thing here. I picked my way to the shoreline, where the ice formed bubbles over the mud, and I jumped at the sound of a mighty roar: "AAAARRRRH!"

I whipped around, and Anthony was hobbling around in the snow by the car, his arms stretched out before him, an orange knit ski mask over his face. "Ax murderer!" he boomed in a deep voice. "Ax murderer on the loose! Run for your life! Ax murderer, ax murderer, ax murderer!"

I laughed. He pulled the mask off his face and shrugged. "This isn't mine." Standing up there in his broad camel-hair overcoat, he looked oddly flat and stiff, like a paper doll. Then he darted back into the car, slammed the door. The engine ripped into life, tires scraped gravel off the shoulder, and the car moved backward, fast. From my place below, I could see Anthony's head facing front, two hands on the wheel, as if he were casually driving forth and not barreling in the opposite direction, back first over the bridge. The car sailed with one huge, sharp sound through the railing; the next thing I saw was the black smudgy underbelly, the axles, the crankcase, the muffler a flat oblong of silver. The car plunged through the frozen surface of the lake, trunk first. Anthony sat inside, his face handsome and bland. He and the car slipped underwater, leaving a hole in the ice like the pupil of an eye.

After being tossed out of college for cheating, Anthony discovered drugs—hard ones. And about a year later I discovered Anthony—unconscious, shirtless, on the floor of his basement apartment. The rescue workers, bending over his limp body, said it was an overdose, and no way, they said, was it accidental.

I'd come by his place that afternoon to see if he'd take me to the spring dance. I didn't think he would. But I'd decided to try him anyway. I wanted very much to go, and no boy had asked me.

So it was me who called the rescue squad. It was me who kept him here. He told me once, after he'd finished rehab and found the job and girlfriend, that he was thankful to me, but I was fairly certain that was a lie.

I was sixteen then. I'm twenty now, and the memory of that April evening I spent at home from the dance still makes me sad. How much I would have loved it, dancing all night with Anthony.

. . .

My right foot now looks a little like a fork with prongs missing. A couple of hunters came along and found me bobbing in the dark water—like one of those Santa-shaped ice cubes that people float in your Coke around holiday time. I got frostbite and those toes had to go.

The car was fished out, Anthony was buried. The pink marble stone reads LOVE LIVES ON. My father wired a large conglomeration of irises and carnations; my mother displayed our high school graduation portraits. My brother's love interest came to the funeral, but I didn't see her again until months later, when she invited me over for a Saturday lunch and I decided to accept. We ate on the patio. It was clear she'd been having a hard time. She looked tired. We talked, a little but not too much, about Anthony. Afterward, she brought out some dresses she'd designed and stitched together herself. "In fact," she said, draping one over a deck chair, then straightening to gaze at me from beneath her soft dark bangs, "let me measure you? I see you in something for the summer. You know—something billowy, maybe, white."

She dug into her sewing basket, and then, deftly, she circled a yellow tape around me, my shoulders, chest, waist, hips. Standing there holding my arms out to either side, I watched the scene's reflection in her sliding glass doors. In the dark window, it looked as if she were hugging me, again and again. The picture made me happy; I smiled at it. "You know, Anthony really loved you," I said.

LADY
LIBERTY

The blade missed my head by the length of a trout. It flashed by hissing; I squeezed my eyes shut. It clattered to the floor by the sink. Then the question became: how do I forgive him? He yelled "Don't leave me, don't—" as I slammed out the door.

The week after Artie lobbed that whittling knife at me, everyone started making a big deal about Lady Liberty. One morning, the Fourth, strangers wandered through the neighborhood wearing foam Statue of Liberty crowns. I watched them from where I sat five floors up at the window of my cousin Warren's living room, carving soap. I did that a lot after I escaped to Warren's place; there wasn't much else I could do, and I was trying to get my mind around Artie's violent act, trying to do some thinking. That's probably what a hobby's for, why people are always saying you should have one. Artie taught me how to carve. He learned it one weekend drying out in the basement of a courthouse in Trenton. We'd practiced carving together from the day I moved in with him until the night I left in a big hurry—about five months total. It doesn't take too long to learn, but I'd guess it needs a lifetime to perfect.

Soap is a surprising material. I prefer wood, but in the week since I'd left Artie, already I'd whittled down a set of wooden spoons from Warren's kitchen into forks, and I'd made a large salad bowl into a dozen pair of dangle earrings for the typesetters at work. But I still had more thinking to do. So by the time Fourth of July rolled around, I was working in soap.

It was midmorning; I was making a turtle out of a bar of Dial, cooling myself in the breeze of the oscillating fan and watching the crowds swim by down on Hudson Street. My heart felt thick and hot like a pit of tar. Of course Artie was at the bottom of it. I'd been falling for someone who, all eyes could see, was not likely as the man of my destiny, and yet he'd become the major factor in my life, my guiding light.

He'd guided me far from my previous life plan. When I met Artie, I was engaged. Now the memory of my ex-fiancé, Jeff, getting ready for his job at The Athlete's Foot, pulling his phony black-and-white referee's stripes over his skinny chest, made me queasy. Artie entranced me—his smile, his whole being—but he'd tried to do me serious bodily harm. This was a devastating concept.

Back behind me in the apartment a door opened. It
was Warren coming out of his room. He was talking to
someone. "Problem is, brunch isn't profitable. It's a
sinkhole. Your hard liquor sits in the morning." A
woman made agreeing noises. I glanced at the door to the
little study where I'd been sleeping, thinking maybe I
could slip in there before they saw me. I didn't particu-
larly want to witness Warren's morning-after manner.

It was too late. Warren came in first, tucking the tail
of his aqua polo shirt into the back of his pants, deck shoes
squeaking on the wood floor. His wire-frame glasses were
perched on top of his head. Warren is a maître d', but on
his days off he dresses like a vacationing lawyer. Following him was a tall woman with truly impressive hair. With
its arches and warm exotic colors, it reminded me a little
of certain flowers, ones that I'd never seen in yards up in
Fishkill, but only in florist shops in the city. The woman's
eyelashes were noticeable from across the room, very
dark and spiky. Her cheekbones were rosy and defined.
She wore a maroon jumpsuit and carried a black silky
dress on a hanger. I recognized that dress; it was the
waitresses' uniform at the restaurant where Warren rules
the roost.

The woman was looking at me, alarmed. "Morning,"
I said. Warren looked up from his grooming. "Claire!
Morning, morning, morning! Come meet Claire!" He
took hold of the woman's elbow and she wobbled a bit
on her strappy heels as he pulled her across to where I was

sitting in a big armchair by the window. She held out a
long hand to me, which I shook, and she said in a bright
questioning way, "You live here?"

"I'm Warren's cousin." She looked relieved.

"Claire's camping out here for a while," Warren
said. "My baby cousin."

"You have those same hazel eyes," she said, tilting
her head a little and smiling at Warren. I couldn't feel too
bad for her. She'd gotten herself into it.

She reached out a hand and patted my hair. "Is that
a perm?"

"Yes," I lied. My curls have always been beyond my
control. That week I had given up the fight. "It's a Toni
home perm."

"What a crime! See this?" She ran a hand carefully
over her hairdo. "I bled for it. Eighty-eight bucks and six
hours in the chair. Listen. Sometime we should give each
other Tonis."

"Sounds super," I said. It felt strange, seeing things
from the reeling-in side instead of being on the hook. She
was pretty attractive; I gave her three weeks. "I'm Janine," she said.

"Of course," Warren said and smiled wide. "This is
Janine." He slid his arm around her waist and gave it a
squeeze. "She's something." He beamed at her. "Ready
to go?"

"You betcha," said Janine.

They hurried off to a party—it was on a yacht, and
exclusively for employees of overpriced Italian restau-

rants. A very big deal. I went back to my hobby. Janine
seemed nice enough, but she was a rube. "Hoping against
hope," I said out loud. The fan, my sidekick, sucked air
and clattered.

The phone was ringing. The turtle was stuck to my hand.
I'd fallen asleep. I was dreaming what I sometimes dream
when I nod off in a sitting position, especially at work.
I'm floating on my back in a gorgeous swimming pool,
but what I don't know is that I'm very close to the wall.
I'm going to hit my head.

The phone was ringing. I answered, and it was Artie.
He got right to the point; he knew he had to. "Watching
the fireworks tonight?"

"I might."

"Will you tell me where?"

"No." His voice seemed to increase the flow of blood
to my eardrums. I could barely hear him.

"I'll probably watch from somewhere down on the
West Side Highway," he said. "I think I'll just walk
down the block."

I stared at a picture on Warren's wall. One of
Picasso's nude women, sprawled on a sofa bed; I didn't
much like it at the moment.

"When are we going to talk?"

"No time soon," I said. I realized something then.
There's me, freshly dropped out of community college,
and there's Artie, forty-five and the creator of the adventures of Nuke-man for the famous comic books, and now

it's me who's saying when we do what. A week ago Friday I would have dyed myself green if he'd told me to. I would have shaved my head.

"You know I'm just around the corner," he said. I sat down on the parquet, realizing that his future was in my hands. I hated this thought. I hung up on him.

The liquor store where Cal works carries one hundred brands of beer. Sometimes it's a little too much. That afternoon I stood there looking at this parade of many nations and pictured a million Arties across the globe, all getting blotto.

I was restocking Warren's fridge. "Bud's on special," Calvin said. "No difference to you, am I right? Only thing you'll drink is Harveys Bristol Cream." He was teasing me. He's the liquor delivery man and rules the neighborhood—a black guy with a flattop haircut and "Montauk Marlin Club" on the back of his windbreaker. Every Saturday, he goes deep-sea fishing. Only one reason to live, he says: to fish the big fish. He delivered that last bottle, the night Artie performed the knife toss.

I paid for the six-pack, and Calvin shouldered a case of beer, saying, "I gotta make a drop. I'll walk with you." We headed out onto Hudson Street. It was a little after five, and the heat had softened. Partying people were pouring in from uptown, Queens, the Bronx, carrying lawn chairs, camera tripods, silver balloons, ice chests, buckets of Popeyes chicken. Every group moved down the street to the beat of its own radio.

"There oughta be a law against this Statue of Liberty shit," said Calvin, dodging a toddler. He shifted the weight of the box on his shoulder, tilting it back so he could look at me. "So how's old Nuke-man?"

"I don't know. I sort of left him."

"Oh, man. Choppy waters."

"Yeah, pretty choppy."

"Well, you're gonna ride it all out, baby face. Just ride it out."

Right then, in the rowdy street, I could have gone on a crying jag and told him everything that had happened, how I was sure my life was in a shambles and I didn't have anyplace to go. Artie had plucked me up from New York State nowhere, and I didn't want to go back. It might have felt good to spill this out to someone. On the other hand, it was no time to get teary eyed. The whole city was throwing a big party.

"Look up there," Cal said, jerking his head toward a building across the street. "On the third story."

"That lady?" She stood in one of the windows—a woman of about fifty, with dark hair. I recognized her from the neighborhood. I'd seen her walking her dog, a Yorkie that snapped at people. Once in a while I'd see her in the grocery store; she wore elegant clothes and bought pineapple. "What about her?"

He swung the case down and cradled it in front of his chest. "Calls the store just about every other Friday night and orders two fifths of Stoli, then answers the door in her nightie."

I looked up at her again. I pictured her alone with her highball, nightie, and yapping Yorkie. She probably thought she was invisible, up there above all the families and sightseers.

"More people around like that than you want to know," said Cal.

We were crossing Eleventh Street, where Warren lives. "I'm turning here," I said. Someone carrying a giant green inflatable Lady bumped into me.

"Watch yourself," Calvin said. Balancing the beer on his hip, he reached out with his free hand and slid the strap of my purse back onto my shoulder. "You come up to my roof later, I got a great view," he said, and kept on walking downtown.

It's true the roof four floors above Cal's rented room looks right over the West Side Highway and right over the river. When I got up there, he showed me the parts of the lumpy surface to stay away from. "Mrs. Berger's ninety-seven. Can't stomp on her head, we gotta give her some peace," he said. It's one of those ancient tenement buildings with a lot of elderly people who've lived there since they were born.

"Well, those firework guys'll make a lot of noise," I said. "Those Italian guys." I sat down on a metal folding chair Cal had brought up. At that point it was absolutely quiet, high up there. It was a real relief, being so near to the dim empty space of the sky. And beyond the rooftop the smooth river slipped under the boats, under the custom cruisers and the U.S. Navy, and out to sea, calm, almost unnoticed amid all the liberty hoopla. I felt my worries cool.

I was thankful to Calvin. Other than him, the only people I'd met in the city were from work, a job Artie got me.

When I met Artie, I was selling rings at Zales and studying part-time at Fishkill Community. He taught my beginning painting class. When I moved in with him, he set me up at *SexLife,* where I paste up the classified ads. It's pretty easy; I deal mainly with the girls in typesetting and advertising, and not with Jorge, the art director, who yells all day long: things like "Bring me a three-column nipple close-up pronto!" Then his assistant has to either find something in the "NIPPLE" file or else crop one off some used full-body shot.

Over on the corner of the roof, Calvin was poking the coals in a crusty old hibachi. A thin silver chain shone around his neck. I could see a nutlike bead dangling just inside the collar of his T-shirt. "What's that?" I said, pointing.

He touched it, a little wooden ball. "This I got recently from a certain Diane. She carries a mahogany sphere in her pocket that she says deflects and absorbs all cramps and stomachaches. The way she sees it, aches and pains float in the air in invisible clouds. Like how a clump of oil suspends itself in the water, waiting to smear some fish swimming by."

"Interesting." I sipped my beer.

"Yes, she's interesting," he said, rolling the hot dogs thoughtfully, smiling to himself. "She was raised in Tampa, Florida."

"Wow," I said. "I see what you mean." But really, I did see. In spite of all the bad, in spite of everything, I knew I still felt that way about Artie—every stupid detail was significant, every scrap of info was a little clue. Why this person, and why me.

The coals were smoky. I walked to the clear air at the edge of the roof, and so did Cal. A reddish color had soaked through the sky and dripped down onto the warehouses across the river, the boats and the water, the chrome on cars. Crowds of people lined the piers and the highway. We stood there, and I pictured this comic-book artist, brown hair frizzed with gray, hunched shoulders, out there too. It was just about nighttime. He was standing with a lot of strangers, waiting for it to get dark.

"Artie's down there somewhere," I said.

"Well, you never know, Claire. Could be you're better off."

"Maybe." There were certainly things I didn't understand. Sometimes we'd just be set adrift in our lovemaking, tossing and dancing out in space somewhere. Sometimes he'd be unable to perform for days, and he'd get up and sit drinking when he thought I was asleep. I didn't understand how I could still want to be lying in that bed. He could have put my eye out, or taken my life.

"He adores me," I said.

Cal shrugged and sipped his beer.

"Now listen," I said. "Artie was really depressed that night, he was tanking up. We're sitting there carving and a TV show comes on, *Love Is in the Air,* about three stewardesses who live in an apartment and have boyfriends and adventures. It's sort of funny so I'm laughing. Then I go to the kitchen for a Coke. When I open the fridge I think of something; I say to Artie in the next room that maybe I should apply to flight attendants' school. I don't want to spend my life at a porno rag, right? So when I come back into the room, Artie stands up from his chair, roars out 'FLIGHT ATTENDANTS' SCHOOL!' and sends that knife flying. Like a missile. It whistled in the air. I heard it."

"Hmm," said Cal. "So you think I oughta try that on Diane."

I drank some beer. "So I was completely in shock for about ten seconds. I'm realizing he could've killed me. I run into the bedroom, throw some clothes into a shopping bag, and go barreling out the door. He was screaming. He was crying."

Calvin finished his Bud and threw the can onto the next rooftop. After a minute, he said, "Who knows what's what?"

"I never liked hearing the buzzer and seeing you in the peephole with a brown bag."

"Yeah."

"But he's not a drunk." I thought of the woman with the dark hair, the one up in the window. "He gets depressed sometimes and he drinks."

"Whatever you say, baby face." He seemed disappointed in me, but maybe that was just what I was hearing. For a while Cal had sort of a yen for me, but he probably didn't anymore. It was my policy to not notice.

He went over to the hibachi and knelt down, stabbed the hot dogs with a fork. I finished my beer and threw it onto the other roof, too. I heard it land with a tiny clank. Down below, an ambulance came whining along West Street. The tar pit was there inside of me again.

By the time we ate the dogs and drank up the rest of the beer, it was dark. Out on the river, the tall ships were strung with colored bulbs. All the boats were lit, and the lights reflected in the water. The statue, in the distance, was surrounded by dazzling white. From where we sat, it might as well have been sculpted out of mint-green Zest.

At Warren's, the heat kept me from sleeping. I was lounging in front of the fan again, putting the finishing touches on the turtle, when the telephone rang. I answered it and Artie said, "I didn't see you at the fireworks!" I could tell he was trying to sound casual and jolly.

"There were three million people there," I said.

"I know." His voice lowered and a long breath fuzzed in the receiver. "I can't tell you how miserable I am. I've been sitting on the sofa, sobbing, wishing I could change the course of history. Claire. Honey. You are my only hope. My last, greatest, and sole surviving hope."

These words he pronounced slowly, in a voice full of feeling and grandeur, the way the President likes to speak. In spite of myself, I warmed to him a little bit. "You tried to kill me," I said.

"I was out of my mind. I had a vision of you traveling far away from me, wearing a polyester scarf, dying in a midair collision."

"No. You blew it. You must think I'm stupid. You ruined everything and I can't come back. No. No way." I closed my eyes so I wouldn't cry.

"Claire," he said. "On our first day together, you taught me to play golf with a Frisbee. Through the whole bloody thing I was thinking, what an extraordinary young woman! I pictured our whole life together. I saw that I could give you a larger life. And I saw that you would be my solace. I knew it."

"I don't want to be your solace." I remembered something my mother had told me. "I am in the prime of my youth," I said.

"I am urging you to believe in me. Think about it, will you, dear?"

"I can't talk anymore." I was sweating; my hair was wet on the back of my neck.

"If you need me, I'm just around the corner," he said, and I put the receiver down.

I went back to the chair by the fan and picked up the turtle again, but I couldn't work on it because my hands were shaking. Out of all the women in beginning painting, it was me he had picked. I never even finished the semester. My grades read *W* for *Withdrawal* in every class.

Later, a woman called for Warren. She sounded uncertain, hearing a female voice answer. She said, "Will you tell him Angela called?"

"No," I said. She waited a few seconds before she hung up.

I didn't hop right out of bed the next morning. It was Saturday. I lay there looking at the dusty light fixture, thinking about Artie's forearms, thinking about their warm and hairy surfaces. My clothes were heaped in the corner.

After a while, I rolled off the cot and walked into the living room. Warren was sitting on the couch, reading the newspaper. Sounds came from the kitchen—clattering pots and pans, then a voice: "How does a western omelet grab you?"

"Sounds terrific!" Warren said. He looked up at me, said, "Good morning!" and then, louder, "Is there enough for Claire, too?"

"Sure thing," cried the cooking voice, which I identified as Janine's.

"Isn't she something?" he said to me, flashing a smile; behind his aviator frames his eyes shone with what looked to me like real affection, maybe even love. Right then I realized: Warren isn't getting some sick pleasure out of breaking waitresses' hearts. He just picks people up the way someone else might pick up a good thriller or a romance paperback. It's so good, you love it so much, that you can't put it down, so you finish it quick, maybe quicker than you really wanted to. You enjoy the whole thing immensely. After it's done, though, you don't treasure it, or ponder over it. You just start a new book.

Suddenly, I wanted to talk to Janine about this. She was cracking eggs into a bowl, wearing a blazing yellow sundress. "Can I lend a hand?"

"Sure! Be a doll and pop some bread in the toaster."

I did that, and then I said to her in a low voice, "I want to tell you something. About Warren."

"Yes?" She turned and smiled at me. I bit my lip; I felt uncomfortable, but pressed on. I needed to know what she would say.

"I just think I should tell you that—" I paused, turning the spongy bread loaf in my hands. "He's got a short attention span. With women."

She poured the beaten eggs into a pan. "Tell me something I don't already know." She gave a girlish chuckle and dabbed at the eggs with a spatula. "Your cousin's been topic number one in the employees' dressing room since about 1983."

I shook my head. "If you already know there's trouble, then how can you forge ahead like that? In the face of certain disaster." My voice sounded high. "By just overlooking everything?"

"I guess you look at it. But there's no such thing as a certain disaster. Just no such thing. I say, 'Janine, you gotta have heart, you could be the one.' People are ripe for change. Happens all the time." She took a step back from the stove. "Now watch how I do this." She grasped the pan and gently shook it, flicked her wrist. The omelet took shape, and she flipped it sideways, then tipped the pan. The soft crescent landed on the plate—Pffft. Absolutely perfect. Inside I felt a slipping sensation. She could be right, I thought.

"I've never been a toe tester," she said, handing me the plate with a pert smile. "I plunge right ahead. That one's a triple-egger."

I took the plate from her. She was making me think. "You seem so nice. I just thought maybe I should let you in on, you know, Warren's history. Because I'm—"

I turned around and the plate hit right against his chest. The omelet slid a little but stopped halfway over the edge.

"What's wrong with my history?" Warren said, scooping the flap of egg back onto the plate. He looked hurt and stunned, as if I'd just thwacked him across the face with a rubber glove for no reason at all.

"Claire's just being a silly sweetheart," said Janine. "She's worried about our future."

His lips curled into a little grin. He looked at me and tousled my hair. Then he went over to Janine, firmly took the spatula out of her hand, and put his arms around her. "Looks bright to me," he said with a dashing smile. She giggled. They started rubbing noses.

I took my plate out to the dining table in the next room. As I sat there waiting, I started remembering things about Warren—after all, I've known him my entire life. He'd seemed to me, when I was a kid, like a character on television, with his cigarettes and white denim bell-bottoms. Then he broke his back slipping on ice in a used-car lot in Fishkill. I went to visit him at Aunt Sue's. He helped me with my homework and I gawked at the pinup on his closet door. Once, I saw my aunt helping him go to the bathroom. I remember how depressed he was during that time; that's probably when I stopped thinking he was the most incredible guy I knew. Since I moved into New York, into his neighborhood, I'd been doing my best to avoid him. Until my evacuation from Artie.

Warren put his plate and some glasses of juice on the table. As he sat down, I said, "You taught me the multiplication tables, you know."

He looked at me, his brows raised, his thin hair uncombed from the night before. His eyes grew faraway behind his glasses. I knew he must be picturing the two of us in his old bedroom: him propped up, torso stiff and white; me with my scraggly ponytail hanging over one shoulder, sitting by his bed with a math workbook spread on my lap.

"So I did," he said, still gazing at me. He picked up his fork and looked down at it, almost shyly. He said, "Anytime, my sweet, anytime."

Then the phone rang, startling us both. Janine hurried into the room, carrying her plate, singing out, "Claire, it's Artie. You must eat quickly, or it loses it fluff."

"Morning," I said quietly when I picked up the extension. Warren and Janine were watching me. Resting my elbows on the sill, I leaned out the open window, listened to his explanations and phrases of love. Looking down toward Hudson, I saw there was more trash than usual in the street, from the Lady's birthday. Then I noticed Calvin, walking beneath the screen of leaves, wearing a red muscle shirt and carrying a small case, a tackle box. I knew he was headed toward the subway. I watched him kick a soda can into the gutter, and then I interrupted Artie. "Hang on a sec." I lowered the phone and leaned a little farther out. "Cal," I called. He nodded up at me and gave a small wave, then kept on his way. "Wish me luck," he called back over his shoulder. I watched him go. Every week he waited, dreamily lost in hoping, thirty-two stops to the ocean.

I lifted the phone back up and pressed it to my ear. "I'm here again," I said. "I'm listening."

LOTS

In the earliest hours of a summer morning, Sid was awakened by delicate noises. Someone was sneaking through his house. He'd been expecting this. He figured that any fugitive killer would consider them the perfect victims, living out on this brand-new street where the nearest neighbors were eight one-acre lots away. He entertained morbid visions of his family in the aftermath of the slayings: his mother would lie in a dark puddle; on her good living room rug. Harry, his brother, would fall in the hallway, silver marijuana-leaf pendant pasted in the blood between his bony shoulder blades; his father would lay sprawled through the opened back door, arms thrown out toward the woods, where he'd been heading to get help or to get away.

Sid would be the lone survivor. He'd give stirring interviews to familiar faces from the evening news.

For security's sake, Sid had stolen a dull, evil-looking scaling knife from his father's tool box and hidden it in the narrow slot between his bed and the wall. Listening to the intruder's soft approach, his father's old knife flashed in his mind. The thought of using it scared him.

The hall light popped on. Sid's brother walked by the open door.

"Hey," Sid whispered loudly.

Harry reappeared in the lighted doorway and stuck his head into the blackness of Sid's room. "Sleep," he said. He vanished, and the hall light clicked off. Harry's door slammed shut. Too loud, Sid thought, for someone who was trying to sneak around. Then he heard his parents, passing down the hall with heavy steps—not the gentle rustle of parents moving through a house that holds their sleeping sons.

The next morning, Harry drove Sid to his summer job at Quick Chicken. Turning into the parking lot, Harry said, "Dad put the car in a ditch last night. Got picked up by Fairfax County cops, drunk out of his mind." He stopped the car at the restaurant's back entrance, leaned across Sid, opened the glove compartment, and pawed cassette tapes.

"Mom and I went to pick him up. He was holding some girl's purse, the asshole."

Sid stared out at the brimming Dumpsters, astounded by this information. Harry turned on the radio. Lifting a stiff arm to the door handle, Sid said, "See you," and staggered out of the car.

. . .

Saturday night a few weeks earlier, Sid had been sitting
on the front steps waiting for Dave Denton, a sixteen-
year-old with a Camaro, to drive out to the house on the
promise of stolen liquor. They would head down to the
end of the street, where a dirt track led through the
woods to an abandoned cargo van, its bare rims sunk into
the ground. That was where they drank.

The front door opened behind Sid, and light spilled
out across the grass. The first-year growth was sparse:
each blade cast a shadow. He turned to see his father step
outside, holding a preparty scotch and dressed up in a suit
a shade darker than the ones he wore to his office at
Calvert Foods. Slicked back with water, his thick, sandy
hair was flat and furrowed. After-shave wafted down to
Sid in a green-smelling cloud.

"What're you doing out here—waiting for a bus?"
his father said.

"Waiting for some people." Sid scooped up a handful
of mulch from the planter next to him and started throwing wood chips out onto the grass.

His father took a sip and crunched some ice. "We're
going to a party in a private room at Clyde's," he said.
"If you need us." He ruffled Sid's hair until Sid ducked
his head away. "I might slip downstairs, though. It's
supposed to be a singles club. What do you think? I look
good?"

Sid turned to look him over, then shrugged. "I guess.
Maybe Mom'll meet some guy at the party." They joked

like this all the time, but it made Sid uneasy. The same uneasiness swept over him when his father stared at women walking by in a shopping mall or on the street. He stared after them openly, without shame, and Sid thought it disgraceful. He pretended not to see.

"Your mother would do just fine. She'd love it. She'd dance with all the men. She loves to dance. I don't." He sipped his drink. "You make your choices."

"I guess," said Sid, throwing bombs of mulch against the ground.

"I guess." His father sighed. Sid smelled the alcohol. He wished Jamie and Wilder and Dave would get there so they could slip out to the van and open up the bottles of gin from Jamie's parents' wet bar.

Sid's mother, in a red silk dress and a tightly curled hairdo, appeared in the doorway. "You're letting bugs into the house, Ed," she said.

"I was just telling Sid how you loved a man who loved to dance. Isn't that true?"

"True enough," she said sharply.

Sid's father finished his drink and tossed the rest of the ice out onto the ground. "Let's go."

Sid's mother bent to kiss her son. "As usual, I don't know where your brother went. If he calls, tell him home by one-thirty?"

"Okay."

She followed Sid's father down the walk to the driveway. Sid watched them pull away. Then he stared across the street at the ragged woods.

. . .

Three weeks after that night, one week after his accident, Sid's father was exiled to a condominium tower downtown. His apartment, rented at a discount from a realtor friend, also served as the building's model unit. On the weekends, young couples trooped through, taking note of the built-in microwave and the black enamel bathtub. Sid's father would call the house and complain. "I worked all my life for that house, and now I'm living in a Bloomingdale's showroom," he'd say to Sid, his voice soggy with alcohol. "Can you explain that to me?"

Sid began high school, and all through autumn the trees around the house shook. Bulldozers were breaking ground on the lot next door. Muddy tracks led up and down the street; a deep foundation was dug. The family beagle begged for scraps from the crew's lunch bags.

Around the time the last leaves blew off the trees, Sid's father began to date Renee Smith, the meteorologist on Channel Five, whom he'd met at remedial driving school. She'd been charged with two counts of DWI; he claimed she was now sober and a terrific person.

Sid's mother did not date. Family friends called less frequently; she often asked Sid or even Harry to go downtown for dinner and a movie on a Saturday night. "A single woman is a pariah out here," she'd say, and Sid guessed it must be true: there wasn't an unmarried man or woman over the age of twenty-two in any of the new houses on the street; people who moved to the neighborhood did so because they were part of a finished, airtight unit.

One blue-black evening in January, Sid wandered into the kitchen and wondered about dinner. His mother was nowhere to be found. The squall of Led Zeppelin canceled out all other sound from Harry's room. Nobody had fed the dog.

Sid poured chow into her dish, spilling it across one corner of the kitchen floor. He marched to the other end of the house and pounded on Harry's door. "Hey. I'm hungry. Let's go to the pizza place," he said, trying to be heard over the music. There was no answer. He banged harder.

"Harry! Shit, will you turn that down?" Sid bashed his shoulder against the plywood door with the full weight of his body. He heard short cracking sounds. "Harry!"

Suddenly, he was furious. Their lives had collapsed. He couldn't stand this disorder. He blinked hard—his eyes stung, his shoulder was aching. He rushed into his room and snatched the knife from its hiding place.

He reeled back across the hall and threw himself against the door again. Guitars shrieked. "Open up, Harry! Open up!"

The door fell back and Sid plunged into the room, the knife flailing in front of him. "Christ," Harry yelled, tripping backward against his desk, nearly knocking it over. Dry brown marijuana leaves and twigs skittered down the glass desktop to the floor. A small plastic scale tumbled and came apart in two pieces.

The knife suddenly awkward in his hand, Sid stared at

the mess. "You pulled a knife on me?" Harry said. "You pulled a knife on me?"

"You idiot," Sid said. "You—"

"You're out of your mind, Sid. I mean it. You're crazed."

Sid let the knife drop to his side. "I was hungry."

The music roared behind him as he walked out of Harry's room. He put the knife back into the toolbox. Drifting into the living room, he turned on the television.

A few minutes later, the front door opened and Sid heard his mother's heels tick along the hallway. "Anybody home?" she said.

"No," said Sid, motionless among the sofa cushions. "We're having dinner at the White House."

His mother entered the living room, sporting a vicious run in her right stocking; her coat with the huge brass buttons like saucers down the front was sliding off one shoulder under the weight of an enormous tote bag. She allowed the bag to slip off her arm, and dropped to the couch. After six months without her husband, she looked older, rumpled, needy. Sid felt contempt.

"Where were you? Lost?" he asked.

"No, I wasn't lost." She unbuttoned her coat. "I was registering for classes. You'll have to get your own dinner on Tuesdays and Thursdays. I'm going to need time."

"Great," said Sid, clutching a throw pillow to his chest. "You screw up your life and I pay for it."

His mother bit off a loose bit of thumbnail, looking at

him. "I'm tired of you," she said. "I'm going to bed."

A pert voice coming from the television made him turn toward the set. "That's right, tonight we'll be using that four-letter word"—the woman smiled mischievously—"S-N-O-W."

"Christ," muttered Sid. But he had to admit she was not unattractive. She was a little like a grown-up cheerleader in a business suit.

The sod sprouted a tender and thick early growth in April. Sid's father drove out one afternoon and walked the perimeter of the yard, from the curb in front to the edge of the forest in the back.

He watched as Sid and Harry played an unfriendly game of one-on-one beneath the new basketball hoop he'd bought them. "That's good sod," he said, kicking the grass with the toe of his old outdoorsman's boots. "Took hold very well. I made a good buy." Sid and Harry barely heard him. "Don't forget to water it when it starts getting hot. Each side of the house."

"Yeah," said Sid, heaving the ball toward the hoop.

"House next door's getting there, huh?" Sid's father shook his head. "Huge, too. Must've cost a fortune."

Sid nodded. "Mom says the guy building it makes TV commercials."

They looked over at the lot. Where there was once a wall of trees, there was now a mud-flat. The tar-papered framework that rose in its center dwarfed their own house. "Well, it was nice while it lasted," said his father. He stuck his hands in the pockets of his old blue windbreaker, looked down, and scraped the mud from his shoe onto the pavement. "I miss living out here, you know."

Harry tossed Sid the ball. "That's it for me."

"Anyone for a ride to the hardware store? We need a new sprinkler head," said their father.

"Nah," said Harry. "I've got homework to do." He glanced at Sid.

"Sid? How about you?"

"No, I'm going out later."

"Who with?"

"No one you know," he said, walking toward the house.

"Well, tell whoever's driving to be careful. They're forecasting rain."

Sid turned as he pushed the door open. "I guess you've got the inside scoop on the weather." He stepped into the house and hurled the ball into the hall closet, cracking the vacuum-cleaner casing. "Great," he muttered. He reached into the closet and turned the cracked side to the wall.

A crew rolled in and tore up the brambles in the southeast corner of the lot next door to make way for a swimming pool. That afternoon, Sid arrived home to find Harry slouched in a patio chair, watching the bulldozers, crying. There was a large hole where the bramble patch had been.

"Looks like it'll be a big pool," Sid said tentatively, eyeing Harry.

"I had Afghani Gold planted out there. What I went through to get that shit. I can't believe it." Harry shook his head, his face damp and puffy. He sniffed and wiped his nose on the sleeve of his dirt-smeared denim jacket.

Sid threw himself into the other chair. The Caterpillars churned and scraped, their gears grinding.

"I'm thinking about this kid I heard about," said Harry. "He went to Lincoln. Listen to this. His mom gets remarried, so when they go on their honeymoon, the kid packs up all the wedding presents, jewelry and silver, china plates, and sells it to a fence in Anacostia. Then he takes off. Just like that. He made it to California, ended up camping out on the beach with a dog."

Living at the edge of the ocean, having a big dog: the picture rushed into Sid like air. The idea was so simple, running away. It thrilled him.

Quiet dropped on the yard. The machines had been cut off; the men climbed down from their cabs.

"It's Miller time," said Harry, watching them file away. He spit in their direction, then looked back toward the sliding glass door. "Mom home?" he said. Sid shook his head.

Harry reached into his back pocket and, from an inner fold in his wallet, withdrew a joint, flattened like a tapeworm. He held it up toward a last crewman, who was locking his backhoe. "This one's for you, garden weasel." He lit it and offered it to Sid. Sid hadn't smoked before, but he took it now. He inhaled deeply; the smoke made him cough, at first, until he felt a tiny hole in his head, open to the sky.

A special announcement was made on the Channel Five news. Weatherlady Renee Smith would marry the anchor from Channel Seven in a ceremony to be broadcast on the *Beautiful Morning* show. A few days later, Sid's father arrived to plant a vegetable patch at the side of the house. Sid agreed to help him for ten dollars. They planted tomato plants, zucchini, and melons, much more than they could possibly use.

Afterward, Sid's father asked his mother if she'd like to have dinner with him. Sid was watching television when his father walked into the room, buttoning his collar, his skin pink from the shower. He opened the liquor cabinet and peered inside. "What happened here?" he said. "I had two bottles of scotch in here. Your mother sure as hell didn't drink them."

Sid fixed his eyes on a commercial for panty hose. "Don't ask me."

"Where's Harry?"

"No clue," said Sid.

His mother walked in, wearing heels, dressed in black. The close-fitting dress, the way her hair was puffed out—Sid knew she'd taken meticulous care.

"What's going on?" she said.

"Harry's been pinching good scotch and there are probably other things missing as well."

"Well, that's your department, Ed. You talk to him. Really, I'm at the end with him."

The two of them gazed into the dusty cabinet. On their faces, Sid saw similar creases and lines. It surprised him that two people could wrinkle alike. They looked tired. Disappointed.

"Let's try to be on time," his mother said.

"I've been waiting for you," his father said.

They waved good-bye to Sid and left in annoyed haste, as always.

After that, Sid's father came often to weed the garden, mow the lawn, and trim dead branches off the trees. In August, when the temperature hit 100 degrees, he moved back into the house.

One evening soon after, the sky was dimming fast and Sid slipped outside, set off walking toward the dirt lane. He thought he might take a sip of the Johnnie Walker he'd hidden under the van's twisted hood. He kicked a rock with his sneakered feet, glad to be out. The house still had an echo, and voices and music bounced hollowly through his bedroom.

As he approached the van, twigs cracked around the far side. He froze. "Dave?" he said. Leaves rustled. No answer. His thoughts scrambled back to the house he'd just left—his father and mother would be doing the dinner dishes and arguing, smoke would be slipping out from under Harry's door. He pictured that scaling knife. If he had it now, would he use it?

The light was nearly gone—and someone was prowling in the woods. Sid yanked himself into a run, stumbling down the lane, out into the street, and he kept going, right into the yard and around the back. Then he saw something, something that made him stop.

His father sat on the patio in dark silhouette. A glass rested on one arm of his chair. He was staring off in the direction of a bright light coming from the yard next door. He hadn't heard Sid's frantic approach. He didn't stir. Sid looked beyond him and saw what so transfixed his father: a woman stretched out along the edge of the swimming pool, her arms extended above her head and her fingers trailing in the water. She had short hair; she was naked.

A bearded man crouched by the side of the pool, filming her with a video camera.

Sid's father sank deeper into his chair. He drained his drink. Sid heard him mutter: ''My God.'' Then he turned in Sid's direction and jerked upright. ''Who is it?'' he asked, squinting into the dark. Sid crossed the patio, the smell of chlorine hanging in the air.

''It's me.'' He put his hand on his father's head and was for a moment surprised: the hair there was very soft, and thinner than he'd thought.

He sat down next to his father. They looked across the yard in silence. Sid enjoyed watching the woman move in the glowing water. Together they heard the man with the video camera calling to her. ''That's the way, my darling,'' he crooned. ''Just beautiful, beautiful.''

THE
NUMBER
OF MY
HEART

Warm dry hours in September when all you hear are flies and maybe somebody flapping a bath mat out a window, it could be 1860 here. Georgia Avenue was called the Seventh Street Road then, just an old dirt lane heading out of the city through corn. But around two-thirty, school lets out and you hear radios and packs of girls screaming, and you know it's now. A little kid named Mojeal comes up sometimes to hang around. He told me once I looked like a man.

I'm tall, is all, I hope—and the uniform: the shiny brown pants too tight across the rear, with pockets sticking out on either hip like ears, the khaki shirt with the arm patch. I know it's not girlish, not very attractive. But then it's not supposed to be. I'm legally allowed to arrest somebody.

Days wouldn't seem so nineteenth century here if I

weren't alone, but after Gunther Lowell had himself transferred to Mount Vernon, they downgraded Fort Stevens to a one-man post. Everything is shrinking back. The Park Service is becoming a lacy thing, mostly holes held together by string.

Gunther's one of a dying breed. Most rangers get into it now for the benefits, or because they want to be a cop but want it bloodless, or, like me, because they enjoy working with people. But Gunther joined the Park Service because a place like Fort Stevens was still alive for him. He could see the Union soldiers snoozing in the shade and Abe Lincoln walking the parapet with the shot whizzing around him. Gunther is being wasted at Mount Vernon, a decorator showcase that doesn't require his interpretive genius. But don't try to telling the Park Service that.

Gunther's wife got sick last spring and that turned his head around. Then began the bad side of our working relationship. He taught me a lot, though, in the year we worked together, and it's a good thing he did, now that I'm the only one here. Occasionally someone will ask me a question—and usually I can tell them what they need to know.

Fort Stevens sits in what is now known as a troubled part of D.C. In the morning, I find signs of unlawful activity scattered in the dust beyond the old earthwork— red and blue vial caps, blackened bits of plastic. On an average day, without school groups, I get less than a dozen visitors, most of them hardened Civil War buffs toting notebooks, poking at the joints of the woodwork, stooping to get a look at the nails in the floor planks. The nails came—or so I was told by a visitor with a magnifying glass and a dainty little broom for clearing dust—from a foundry in Shrive, Pennsylvania, that also made a deadly kind of bullet called a ripper. (Gunther told me once that Civil War trivia reflects the infinite nature of the universe. A billion small details add up to incomprehensible violence.)

Then, yesterday, something out of the ordinary happened. Around 2:00 P.M. I was up in the hut listening to the all-talk station, wiping the windows down with paper towels and a vinegar solution. I'm enjoying a small sense of well-being as the windows go from crusty to clear. And then, between strokes, I see through the window a guy approaching, a young black guy with a fiery pink-and-orange sweat suit. This guy is hurrying up the knoll but still managing to stay in stride, a stride that spells cool in this neighborhood. And right away I'm nervous.

I toss down my wad of toweling and step out of the hut, which is set into the restored general's command post. By now, the guy's scurrying up the earthwork. Members of the public are supposed to keep to the walkways, but I decide not to say anything to him; I just watch, my mind leaping back to the hut, to my billy club hanging from the doorknob, to the phone on the desk. But I just wait there, at the top of the battlement, watching him scramble up, looking down at the dark crown of his head, and I realize suddenly what a clear shot they had, those Yankees. BOOM—right through the top of his skull, down through the rebel's neck, straight into his pounding heart.

When he's closing in on the top, so close I can see sweat shining on his neck and the tag on the inside of his jacket collar, I say, You're supposed to use the Quinary Street entrance, sir.

He looks up at me with a squinty grimace against the sun, his teeth even and white. His fingers are dug, claw-like, into the soft, sloped turf. He closes one eye and says, Sorry, hey. Didn't know.

He scuttles over the edge, and I see he's got dirt on the knees of his sweatpants. He brushes it off, then straightens up. I'm backing away in tiny steps toward the hut. Just in case. We never see many guys from the neighborhood up here.

He wanders over to me and grins and says, I've been wondering about what goes on here.

This is Fort Stevens, I say. At the base of his throat, a silver pendant reads, X-RAY. I'll give you a pamphlet—

You get bored up here? You're alone up here, right?

It's not bad, I say, standing my ground then, tucking my hair behind my ears; was he smirking at my uniform? He turns and walks to a bench under the hut windows, spits, shoves his hands in his pocket, and stretches his legs out. They're short legs, on a long body. He's about twenty-five, I think.

I should bring my little brother up here, he says. Might be educational.

Sure, I say. We like to get kids up here.

Who's we? He looks at me. His eyes are almond shaped, slightly slanted, with long lashes.

I shrug. Park Service.

Park Service. He nods, seriously. Parks for the people.

That's the idea, I say.

So how many people you get up here?

Not so many. I kick the dust with my block-toed ranger shoes, and I wonder what this guy's up to, if he's up to anything at all. I keep my hands in my pockets, my elbows loose.

My name's James, he says, rising from the bench, swinging his arms restlessly. He steps toward me, extending a hand. I take it, and he grasps my hand tightly, giving it one hard shake and dropping it. Then he steps back, glances at my name tag. That your first or last? he asks.

Last, I say.

Miss Morris, how tall're you? Six feet?

I feel my face go hot. I feel that old high school shrinking in my shoulders, my knees. I answer with the same old lie. Five eleven. Not that it's your business, I add. But his interest flatters, relaxes me a little.

He steps backward into the cool of the hut's eaves, leans against the wall, and pulls out a green-barreled ballpoint from his jacket pocket. You a ballplayer? he says. You shoot? He sticks the pen behind his ear.

Yeah, I used to, I say.

You ought to. Ladies' ball's gonna be big money one of these days.

So do you have any questions about the fort? I pick up a cigarette butt, drop it into an ash can. I try to invest myself with federal authority.

Some law against me talking to you, Lady Morris? he says, pressing his hands open against his chest. Some law I don't know about?

I heave a sigh. No. I turn and head around the corner, back into the hut. I begin swabbing the windows again. James puts his face really close to the other side of the glass and waves, the close-fingered flapping wave of a child. Then he sits down on the bench, pulls a small notebook from his pocket and the pen from behind his ear, and begins to write. The back of his head is almost touching the glass. Paper towel in hand, I'm hovering over his shoulder, the whorls of his hair just a few inches away. Then the phone rings, making me jump.

It's my mother. Hearing her bright hello sends a jolt through me; it's jarring, like overhearing yourself on tape. She's been gone for a week, and it's the longest we've been apart in ages. She chatters excitedly, telling me the news: Lisa just had the baby, he has a collapsed lung like they thought he would, but he's breathing fine on a respirator. They'll be able to take him home in a couple of weeks, she says. Mom sounds so happy and so close, though she's way off in San Diego, where my sister, Lisa, moved with her husband, Rodney the navy man. I'll give everybody your love, she says, even Rodney. Behind her voice I think I hear the splashing of a fountain. I wish I was there, I say. The apartment's big for one person.

It is, isn't it? she says. How's the dress coming?

She's been teaching me to sew, and I'm trying my first solo project, pink velvet with a boat neck, for the Park Service Christmas party. It's slow going, I say.

Well, plenty of time, she says, still months to go. She promises she'll take a look at it when she gets back next week.

After I hang up, the thick smudged air here feels heavier. I step outside and around the corner of the hut. I fold my arms across my chest and survey the grounds. An old lady and her old beagle move slowly through the crabgrass on one corner of the lawn, and like he does every day, the beagle lifts his leg and pees on the wooden Park Service sign. Long clouds waver like grayish eels on the horizon, beyond the farthest roofs. My sister just had a baby named James, I say.

Just now? James asks. I turn to him; he's looking up from his pen and notebook. Honest? he asks.

Well, they named him James a while ago, but he was just born now. A display board about artillery tactics is planted on posts in the yard a few feet from the hut. I run my hand across the warm Plexiglas covering and my palm comes back dusty.

They knew it was a boy in advance, then, James says.

They had the tests, yeah. I scuff back to the hut, find a big sponge, fill a bucket in the rust-striped sink.

I lug the bucket, sponge bobbing within, out to the display. James watches from the bench. You clean a lot, he says.

I know. Glancing back at him, I see he's sitting with pen poised on paper, as if he's taking notes on the scene. I slap the sponge against the Plexi, push it to and fro in fat arcs. It passes the time, I say.

You're like a cleaning lady.

It's only *part* of the job. My shirttail tugs free as I stretch to reach the corners. I drop the sponge and turn toward James, one hand slipping back to tuck the shirt in.

He's gazing at me. I bite my lip, trying to decide what to say. I think I need an explanation for your sitting here, I tell him. Not looking around or anything.

Okay. He scratches the hair above his ear with the ballpoint, smiling faintly. I'm not here to look around, he says. I'm hiding out.

Great, I think. Now I'm scared. But I keep a cool look on my face. Who're you hiding from?

He rubs a hand over his nose and mouth, stretching his eye sockets downward. Some friends of mine trying to kill me.

How do you know? I ask. He looks a little frightened, too, I realize—the sweat beading along his hairline. I start noticing the sound of far-off ambulance sirens, the smell of burning trash coming from somewhere up Quinary Street.

A sister of one of these guys tipped me off, he says. So I skipped out my building through the back, and I thought of this place. He smiles up at me. It's perfect, too, he says.

Yeah, it's a fort, I say. Designed to protect.

Right, a safe place. He bites the tip of his pen and studies me. You want to know why they're after me?

I stand and look at him for a good long time. We lock eyes. Not really, I say to him.

So you're not afraid of trouble, he says, frowning. His lips are wine-colored.

Not really. I turn to pick up the bucket.

I was writing my last will and testament, he says. Want me to leave you something?

Nope. I swing the bucket and tip it toward the ground, the water splattering against the dust in a muddy burst. The empty pail knocks against my knee and I realize that my hands are shaking, my legs are shaking, my thighs are tense and weak.

Somehow I make it back into the hut. I think I hear James saying, You okay? Pulling the door closed behind me, I drop the bucket and lower myself to the wobbly office chair, lay my head on the desk, and cry into the blotter.

Now, in the calm of today, I know what brought that on. I see now. That was the first time I'd been on the post alone, with a man, since Gunther. And even though this person was different from Gunther in every respect, it was the stillness, the eyeing of each other, and maybe the thickness of the fortifications around us that brought the afternoons with Gunther back to me.

My face is hot, pressed against my arm, and behind my burning eyelids, flurries of orange snow stream by as

I sob. Gunther's hairy legs with his khakis down around his ankles, the white cotton shorts worn thin. It makes me so ashamed.

When his wife's sickness began, he used to go out to his car and wail in the afternoons; I'd stay away from the south wall, which overlooks the parking lot, after the first time I saw him down there with his big hands flat on the dash, his pale face distorted, the mouth all stretched and rubbery. When he came back up—and it would be just minutes before five now, just minutes before gates-locked, pink stripes of light falling across the old timbered walls of the hut—he'd come back with those red planets for eyes, but his face would be dry.

I'd bustle around then, writing in the logbook, sweeping, maybe adding up the petty cash, trying not to make him feel embarrassed, but I'd steal looks at him as he sank into his desk chair, and my heart wanted to cry out, Don't worry, please don't be so upset. Can I tell you I'd never seen a man cry before, I'd never seen a man with blazing weepy eyes like that? My father, never—not when he left Mom, not before. I have no brothers. Once, I saw a guy in my high school cry when the boys' varsity lost a big league meet. That's it.

I should have reported Gunther, of course—because he started sometimes to take pills on the job, heavy pills, taken from his wife's supply. He tossed them down with orange soda when he thought I wasn't looking.

But I didn't report him.

I blame this partly on my last boyfriend, the ROTC

man. After we graduated, he was assigned to an air fleet in Greenland. He loved me, he said, he promised he'd write. And he did for a while, but then he met another woman. In Greenland! That was devastating. I'd invented an entire future complete with officers-club balls, and now I was reduced to the realities: living with Mom in Alexandria, watching television late at night. And working for the Park Service.

Mom was a great comfort to me then, as always. She talked to me about Dad, about how it was amazing they lasted the nine years they did, considering his personality problems, and I talked to her about the ROTC guy, about what a snake he was. But I never talked to her about Gunther.

Gunther has short hair, brown and soft, and great, broad shoulders, and he's not too old, only thirty-seven. One morning after we'd been working together a few months—shortly after my heartbreak—I saw him replaying General Early's invasion for a group of German sightseers; they gawked as he bounded across the battlements, sweeping his arms north and south to show the movements of horses and troops, dodging imaginary sniper fire. They snapped his photograph and afterward pressed around him to shake his hand. He'd held me enraptured, too. After that, I started to feel a little shy around him; I bought a new mascara and started to wear earrings again. Of course I didn't intend to do anything about it—but when he would sit talking on the phone or filling out reports, I would gaze at his back. I could almost feel his shoulders beneath my hands, solid as the sun-warmed earth.

One frigid February afternoon, he trudged back from his car and sat hunched there at the desk, staring down with red-rimmed eyes at the week's accounts, and I went over and put my hands on those shoulders. It didn't take nerve—I did it without thinking.

Half a minute must have gone by when he tilted his head and rested his warm, stubbly cheek on the top of my left hand. I pulled the chair around, lowered myself to my knees, and hugged him. He touched my hair and groaned. Then I turned my face up and saw that his eyes were wet and dark. I kissed him. A lot, small pressing kisses all over his face and neck. His ears. And he more or less took it from there. He eased me down onto the floor, buried his face in my neck. And whispering, muttering, Jeannie, Jeannie, Jeannie, his voice choked with love.

Of course, my name isn't Jeannie. It's Gwen, and Jeannie was his wife, and she was dying. Cancer of the stomach, like a rippler inside her.

We made love six times in three weeks—always waiting, except for that first time, until after closing, when the gates were locked. And after each time, he'd get up from the floor, slowly straighten his clothes, and say, This is wrong, this is absolutely evil. I know, I'd say. Then we'd get into our cars and I'd drive down Georgia Avenue, cut south through the city and across the river on the flat, ugly interstate bridge, and think how scary, how sick this is, what I'm doing. Then I'd turn on the radio and be happy all the rest of the way home.

Friday, closing, in the third week, Gunther told me he'd asked for and received a reassignment to Mount Vernon. Then he headed down to his car and drove away. I haven't heard from him since. A few months ago, in June, a condolence card was tacked up in the departmental office downtown, with a felt-tip on a chain and a little note: FOR GUNTHER LOWELL ON THE PASSING OF HIS WIFE, PLEASE SIGN. I wrote something stupid: With sympathy, Gwen.

I've always hated the name Gwen. It sounds to me like a question—When? When?

Then James is knocking on the window. Hey, he says when I look up. He's bent over, one hand hooked on the top of the window frame, peering in at me. Why're you crying?

I rub my eyes hurriedly; my embarrassment heats my face even more. I try to ignore him, but he's gone from the window, and a moment later the door to the hut flaps open, and he strolls right in, well, steps in. There's really not room to stroll.

Lowering himself into a rickety folding chair, he leans toward me, elbows resting on knees. Talk about it, he says.

Public's not supposed to be in here, I say, sniffing, picking up a smelly sweatshirt from the lost-and-found carton under the desk and wiping my face on it.

It's a fine afternoon then, he says. Come on outside.

I follow him out. The sun's sliding lower into the dirty haze out beyond the doughnut bakery's roof. Behind us, in the eaves of the ammunition hold, pigeons flutter and murmur.

It's a man, right? he says.

No. I frown at him. My sister's baby has a collapsed lung. He's struggling right now for every breath.

Yeah? That's bad, bad. He shakes his head and looks at the ground, hands on his hips. You know I was an X-ray tech in D.C. General. Capital of sick babies, that place is.

I move to straighten some leaflets in their box by the hold's door, next to where he's standing. I smell faint traces of after-shave, minty, mild. So how come you aren't working there now? I ask.

Cuts. He scans the horizon with a resigned look on his face. The drawdown. That's what's happening now, he says.

Yeah, I sigh.

Would you maybe do me a favor? he says, dropping to a squat.

I look at him. Depends.

Go take a peek and see if you spot a big red Mercedes-Benz close by here. He smiles up at me encouragingly. Just take a look, he says.

I cross to the edge of the east slope, out from behind the ammo hold. A fat, tomatolike car is rolling slowly down Quinary. I look back to James. Yeah, I see it.

Diesel engine, he says. He shakes his head and drops

onto his rear, arms on his knees and his long hands dangling. You always hear those cars coming.

While I'm watching, the car swings into an alleyway. A few moments later, I spot it again at the corner of Quinary and Park, pausing at the light. It noses onto Quinary and starts trawling down it again.

When I turn to James again, he's tugging a fluorescent plastic watch on a string from inside his jacket collar. What time you close? he asks. Five?

Yeah.

He purses his lips, looking unhappy. Ten of, he says. Gotta make a plan.

Why're they after you? I say, turning away from him. I coil a garden hose and hang it up on its bracket.

Money, he says. I owe them a lot of money.

I glance over at him. He shrugs, eyes sad. I made a mistake, but I forgive myself, he says. He spits on the ground and shivers with a small laugh.

Plucking the liner from the trash barrel near the fort's entrance, I note the blurts and whines of the trucks downshifting on Georgia Avenue, the rolling whispers of cars. Rush hour has begun. I twist the top of the bag into a fat knot and toss it by the gate. James is watching my every move, but neither of us speaks.

Back in the hut, I pull down my purse from the shelf it shares with a stained, silolike coffee thermos Gunther forgot; I think some coffee's still in there. Rummaging in my fringed leather bag—a gift from my mom—I find a plastic-backed mirror and peer into it, dropping into the

desk chair. My eyelashes are blond and my eyes are
blue—peppermint drops, Mom says—and when I cry,
my lids swell puffy and pink. They don't look so teary,
though, I decide now, and I take a blue eyeliner pencil
from the purse and run it around the rims, blinking.

I hear James walking outside, his sneaker soles
crunching in the gravel yard. I lean back, tilting the chair
to peer out the door. He's pacing to and fro with his face
open to the sky, lips pressed thin and tight, his hands
clenched behind his head. He reminds me of old pictures
I've seen of Rebel prisoners of war being marched out of
Vicksburg. He looks over and catches me sitting there
with the eye pencil still up by my face.

I tuck the things away, hook my bag over my shoulder, and lock the door behind me. James stops his march,
hides his hands in his pouchy pockets. You look nice, he
says.

I've got to close up now.

He drops his gaze, rubs his chin against a sharp,
nylon-clad shoulder, then meets my eyes. Let me stay the
night here, why don't you.

Well. His lashes flutter an instant, and I think: this
move could get me in big trouble. Mom would say I was
crazy, out of my mind. But she's gone.

All right, I say. I raise my hands and flick my hair out
from the back of my shirt collar. I'll leave the toilet
unlocked.

Fine, he says. I appreciate it. He smiles and looks at
the ground.

I grab the knot of the trash bag with one hand and pull the thick wooden gate shut behind me. So long, says James.

See you.

The flowers in the landlady's garden aren't standing up to September—they're going weak-kneed, slope-shouldered, their pie faces folding. But still, the purples, reds, greens, glow at me through the dusk like dyed gravel in a fish tank. After my commute, I gaze at the garden from our second-story window and eat a bowl of spaghetti. There's a breeze ruffling through the screen, a still-summery breeze, but trimmed with a coolness. The chill makes me think about how there's a man in the fort, and thinking of this makes my throat tighten—so many things could go wrong!—so I try to force all thoughts from my mind. My eating sounds loud, without Mom here to talk with.

When I finish, I go to my bed and pick up the phone, dialing my sister's place in San Diego. Rodney picks up.

Congratulations, Daddy, I say to him.

There's one person we haven't heard from. Your dad. He snorts. I won't hold my breath.

How's James? I ask.

Okay—they say he's doing fine, but I'm asking all who will to pray for him. You ready to help us out on that, Gwen? When's the last time you spoke to the Lord?

Recently, I think. Not long ago. At this, he exhales a long breath that floods my ear. Is my mother there? I ask.

Okay—you stay on the line, I'll just go get her. His voice is polite and bullying, even from the far coast. Rodney grew up on a bean ranch out there, near Bakersfield. He's taken my sister's life in hand. He pities her, child of a broken home.

Hi sweetie, my mom trills when she gets on the phone; she's so tickled about the first grandson. Lisa and Rodney's girls are precious to her, but Mom never had a boy of her own. She tells me about the baby's eyes, blue to stay, she thinks, like mine, and about how Lisa looks— really blooming, she says: half an hour after delivery she was doing her makeup—and while I'm listening, I realize that she considers this birth a late-in-life pleasure and she's lapping up every drop. Mom's sixty-nine years old. She got married at forty-one.

Now I ask her, Mom, listen, this is a funny time, but when you were alone so long, a single person, did you ever get desperate?

She's silent; I wish for a second I could see her, brushing her trim gray hair back with her fingertips.

I was always desperate, she says. Always, always. Until now. Now I'm fine.

Oh. I sigh into the phone.

Gwennie, Mom says, as soon as you forget about that ROTC fellow, the day you let that go, a new man's going to come along and that'll be that. I mean it, sweetie. But you've got to get that other boy out of your head first.

All right, Mom. I'm going to try, I say, and I think,

there certainly are parts of me she doesn't know, she doesn't even know they exist. And I realize I'm not going to mention James.

When I hang up, I'm giddy all of a sudden, because I'm realizing how very alone I am in this apartment, maybe in this life, and how deep solitude is, how bottomless. I stare at the floorboards, the grain of the wood, a cloud pattern between my feet—and I wonder, what is the number of my heart?

In my closet, I push impatiently through my clothes until I find what strikes me. I tug off my uniform slacks and shirt and pull on a black silk blouse, short-sleeved, and then the black sequined miniskirt I bought once for New Year's. I step into black flats with bows on the toes.

At the record player, I flip through my small collection until I find something pounding, something like the music that drifts through the air around the fort. I slap it onto the turntable, run over to the mirror by my closet, fluff up my hair as best I can, and start to dance— manically, much crazier than I'd ever dare outside my bedroom. I flip my hips and throw my hair around, wagging my arms over my head, kicking my feet up in back, wiggling my behind. And I watch in the mirror. But I don't see myself there—I'm seeing beyond my image to where James is dancing with me, in a kind of funky black way that I've seen on television, nodding his head, jutting his hips.

I'm spinning, swiveling, stomping; my arms feel like

they might come loose and go flying across the room. And James is there, too. And I close my eyes and I'm floating, flying, straight through six songs.

But then the record ends. I open my eyes. The vision of James in the mirror is gone. So it's just me, panting, with messed-up hair.

This is pitiful, I say out loud, breathing hard. The tonearm clicks upward and glides to its rest.

I kick off my shoes and sit down on the bed. I look at the sewing machine in the corner, the velvet in a pile on the floor. Pulling myself up again, I go over and pick up one of the odd-shaped panels. This geranium medium-weight will make a lovely winter dress, the saleswoman had told me and Mom. Very feminine, she said, looking up at me. I run my palm across the soft cloth, making the shades change light to dark, back and forth. I conjure up the yellowed index card tacked to the wall of the hut, above the desk. It's stuck there with a blue pushpin, and it reads, in neat caps: GUNTHER AT HOME. Plus a number, which I've never called. Now I drop the fabric and go to the phone.

When the ringing begins, my heart thumps again, even more heavily. I squeeze my legs together.

Hello, Gunther says.

Hi, I say, breathless, trying to sound steady. Gunther, it's Gwen Morris.

Hello, Gwen.

Television or radio is playing in the background at his

house. My insides are tumbling. I try to take a deep breath. I was just wondering how you are doing.

Oh. All right, I guess. How are you? His voice is flat, giving me nothing.

Really good. I bite my lip and close my eyes. The reason I called is, I'm really sorry. And I thought you might like dinner sometime, or anything. A movie.

At this moment I want more than anything to hang up before I hear his answer. I curse myself.

I don't think that's a good idea at all, he says, his voice rising, discomfort making him stammer. There's an edge of anger as he says, I don't entirely blame you, but—

You can blame me, I say, cutting him off. It's okay. I really understand. I hang up.

I roll myself into the checkered afghan my mother made for me, in special colors to match my sheets. Lying facedown on the bed, my head covered, my body co-cooned, I whisper: James. James, James in the fort, did you ever feel so alone?

I bolt up at six-thirty in the morning, naked—sometime in the night, I'd flung off my disco clothes—and I think right off of him. I hurry through a shower, pull my wet hair back in a ponytail, throw on a clean uniform, tie up my ranger shoes.

The early sunshine is brittle, a crisp wind snapping at my shirt. I unlock the car door and slide in, feeling jumpy. The slippery seat is cold through my thin gabardine pants.

Traffic's still light, and I cross town without a hitch. I pull into a drive-through and buy two coffees and two pancake breakfasts. When I slip out at the fence to unlock the big gate, the fort and the neighborhood are perfectly still, asleep; the only sound is the metal cable clanging against the bare flagpole beyond the east side of the fort. The flag was stolen weeks ago; I'm still waiting for another from downtown.

I climb the walkway through fields of grass that look especially green in this golden light—and it strikes me once again as I hurry along how terrible it is that so many people don't know about Fort Stevens's vital significance to the lives we live today—that the rebel army came within a half mile of taking Washington and, probably, winning the war. Way up near Brunswick, Maryland, in 1864, blustery General Early and his men crossed the Potomac then marched down Rockville Pike, where we all buy our discount shoes and get our TVs fixed. The Yankee generals heard about the approach too late, and by the time they mustered troops, the Confederates were heading straight up the Seventh Street Road toward the White House.

They were stopped, of course, at my fort. It was the only battle of the whole war that Abe Lincoln observed personally. He rode out, along with a lot of other D.C. residents, in his buggy. Some historians say he almost got hit by a cannonball, standing exposed up on the north wall, and some soldier yelled, Get down, you fool. Other historians say that's just a tale.

But now I'm unlocking the fort gate, easing it open, and all I can think is, Maybe he's dead. Stop it, I tell myself, he's asleep on a bench.

Dust hangs in the sunlit yard, stirring, and I see a flash of orange disappearing over the grassy top of the far battlement. I run toward it, still holding the breakfasts, coffee spilling through the bottom of the bag. I scurry up to the top of the mound. James is sliding, tumbling down the other side.

Hey! I call. Hang on a second.

He stops himself with some effort and looks back, mouth open, chest heaving. Oh, he says. He climbs a few feet back toward me. I thought maybe it was a janitor or manager or something. Didn't think you'd be coming so early.

I was a little worried.

Thought I wrecked the place. He nods. I cleaned that toilet. You'll like that.

I brought you breakfast, I say, holding up the soggy bag to show him.

Nah. I need to get going now.

My heart drops. Him going. I thought we'd eat together, at least. Where're you going?

Down to some friends in Richmond.

Oh, the capital of the Confederacy, I say, trying to make conversation, trying in my dumb way to hold him.

Yeah, I know, he says, pulling up a handful of grass, gnawing on it. Dull place. You got a sweet roll or something you can toss me?

Pancakes, I say, shrugging.

Yeah, too messy, he says. He looks around. Got to get to the bus station, he says.

I could give you a ride.

Yeah? He scratches his head, squints up at me. In the sunlight, dusty streaks shine on his left cheek and in his hair.

Then, a low thrumming sound drifts up from behind me, and we both shift our glances toward the east lawn. A battered yellow car rolls into view on Quinary. James looks up at me again. So you'd give me a ride? he says. Jesus, I was lucky to run into you, I guess.

Yeah, I'm a lifesaver, I say, and I feel the bright rays, not just warming my back and shoulders but pouring into my body and streaming molten right through my heart. I really don't mind. I shrug.

Then I notice that the yellow car has stopped and a big black man in a Redskins parka has jumped out, and he's holding his arm stiffly inside his coat as he runs across the wide lawn toward James. My eyes go wide, my lips part—James darts a glance over his shoulder. Next thing, he's running, his arms flapping as he bounds down the hill, finally hitting the sidewalk, his steps ringing in the morning silence.

The other man stops halfway across the lawn, pulls his hand from inside his coat, and points a small handgun at James's shimmering orange back. A sharp crack pricks my eardrums. I drop to the ground, behind the earth wall, my head pounding, but I hear James's feet skittering across the gravelly street. I peer up again; the man is still chasing. From behind, he looks fat, his thighs thick in white trousers. The parka's fur-trimmed hood bounces from shoulder to shoulder as he runs. James rounds the corner of Park Street and disappears beyond the crumbling façade of the sewing-machine store.

A woman, very small, only just visible behind the wheel, is driving the yellow car. She pulls up behind the fat man, and he settles into the passenger seat unhurriedly. The car sputters off around the corner and it's gone, too.

I slide back down the earthen wall and shakily cross the yard to the hut. I smell my own sweat. I sink into the chair and shut my eyes for a moment, then call the precinct and tell them an armed man is driving with accomplice in a yellow Impala east on Park, first three letters of license plate are *P-L-E*.

They thanked me. Then I ate both of the coffee-soaked breakfasts. Then I tugged the blue tack from the wall and tore the card with Gunther's telephone number into two halves. I strolled down to the Dumpster, reached over its greasy rim, and dropped the two scraps in. Kids were on their way to school by then, and a group of little boys walked past, trying to set one another's pants on fire with a lighter they'd found. When I took it away from them, they cursed at me.

But now school's in and it's quiet, with the riffling trees and the September heat. And I'm sitting up here in the highest point of the fortifications, where the lookout

first saw the flashes and dust of an invading army at the
far edge of a field. I look over the patched tar rooftops and
dirty streets, hoping nobody's bleeding at this moment in
some oil-stained parking lot, hoping he's making his way
south. Maybe he's on the bus right now, rolling down
through Virginia. Maybe he's thinking again how he's glad
he met me.

TRY
HARD
TO BE
GOOD

Jackie Ferco waited for the Rose Bowl to be over. She wished Stu would hurry up. She sat on the frayed plaid couch in the front room, watching the afternoon creep across the yard, watching the snow turn bluer and bluer. She waited, she combed her wet hair. Her suitcase sat by the door, next to an umbrella stand stuffed with the junk mail of housemates who'd moved on. Finally, she saw his car coming down the street, shining like the icy trunks of the trees. So here they really were, going.

She went to the door to meet him. He stamped in with snow on his boots. "They lost it on a wild throw," he said.

"What do you know," said Jackie.

"Last throw of the game."

"And what'd your dad say?"

"About us? Said we're screwed going like this with no

job at the end of the line.'' He took off his knit cap and flattened his dark hair with his hand. ''He said the grass is brown all the time out there.''

''Isn't that like him,'' said Jackie. She tossed her comb into her purse and snapped it shut. ''I'm ready to go.'' She hugged him very hard, his down jacket still cool from outdoors, her socks getting wet in his melt puddles. Stu took her suitcase, she put on her boots and coat and mittens, and they went out into the late-day darkness to the car. All down their block, the street was empty, old bushes and houses lumped with snow, the front yards deserted and a few streetlights coming on.

Jackie walked over to her side of the black sportscar and put her hand on the door handle. Then she fell. Her feet simply slid out fast from under her body; she flew up and flopped down on the snowy driveway. She ended up with her face by a tire. She lay there for a moment, wondering why no one in that house ever shoveled anything.

Stu said, ''What the hell?'' then walked around the car and looked at her. Jackie sat up; one hip felt mashed but she knew it was okay. ''I'm all right,'' she said. Grabbing on to the handle of the car door, she lifted herself to her feet again.

''There goes my perfect record,'' she said. ''First time this winter.'' All over town during those long snowy seasons, they'd see people tipping over into slushy puddles along the curb, falling down in the middle of the street. It was something each person would keep track of

over a winter, how many times he or she went down.
Jackie's friend Ellen Pratt had once fractured her pelvis in
a sidewalk slip.

Stu went back around and they got into the car. Soon
they were on the interstate, west-southwest. Stu said
they'd stop for coffee when they crossed out of Michigan,
just to give themselves something to shoot for. He turned
on the radio. They listened to the guitars and the drums
and the low blast of the heater. Jackie hummed along with
the music, and Stu lit a cigarette.

"Strange, starting a trip in the dark," said Jackie.

Stu nodded. "We'll go as far as we can tonight and
then we'll start fresh in the morning."

"Okay." She hummed a bit more, then said, "I like
the sound of that, 'start fresh.' "

She rolled down the window a crack, and the air of
the frozen farmlands brushed the top of her scalp and
smoothed some strands of her hair back against the headrest. The highway was badly lit and she thought it must
be tough driving. She looked over at Stu, who was staring
down the road, either paying really close attention or not
paying any at all.

"What's going on with you and Randall Harper?" is what
he'd said to Jackie the night before.

"What?" she'd said; she finished her drink. The people they shared the old house with had gone off to spend
the holidays with their families. Just Stu and Jackie were
there, having scotch and sodas in the peeling yellow

kitchen, getting ready for a New Year's dance at Joe's Star Lounge. It was their third year going to that party together. Stu sat back, his body hiding the metal-and-vinyl kitchen chair, a glass of coppery scotch resting on one knee. He'd been more silent than usual; Jackie had noticed this. Stu's silence was one of the things that kept her with him, because it seemed somehow wise and comforting.

But now he sat looking at Jackie in a way that made her nervous. "I saw Harper coming out of the house today," Stu said. "I was driving by. He was standing on the porch, zipping his coat."

Jackie frowned and watched the sweating tumbler on Stu's knee. She thought that someone else, talking about her and Randall Harper, might have taken that cocktail and sent it crashing against the far wall.

Sitting there in their kitchen, she wished with all of her might that she could undo her wrongs, somehow, take back some of the burden she'd laid on Stu. How he got out of bed in the morning with all that, she couldn't imagine.

"I wish I knew what he was doing over here," said Stu. "Or I wish I didn't know."

"Stu," she said, looking down, smoothing a hand over her skirt. "You're truly the best person I've run across yet—ever. And if I've been"—she sighed—"seeing Randall, or whoever else, it's for all the wrong reasons."

Jackie rubbed her winter-raw knuckles. The thought

came to her that as long as she was in this town, she
would never stay on a true course with Stu. That's how
she saw the situation. A person could be led astray by all
the worn tracks here, the old paths you'd rediscover by
chance when you were just happening by. She didn't try
to explain this to Stu; it was just a conviction she had.
Randall, and the others, the old boyfriends—these people
were snagged in her brain like snatches of old songs. Just
hearing a few notes could irresistibly call up the whole
tune. How could she explain that to Stu?

But maybe he understood it, somehow, because when
Jackie said, "I think if we went somewhere new, if we
weren't here . . ." he nodded his head slowly.

"Yeah, we should leave for good," he said, lifting his
glass. He tipped it back and drained it.

That night, the last night of the year, Jackie watched
him drinking with his buddies, telling them about his
plans. She was mystified. She was a little amazed that he
was willing, after all, to give her one more chance.

They drove until late and then stopped at a motel in
Indiana. Jackie was running the bathroom sink, getting
ready for bed, when Stu said to her from the other room,
"You know, when I saw Harper standing on that porch,
I told myself, that was it, I was through. I felt almost like
I could kill you."

"But you didn't," said Jackie.

"Nope. I think this is going to be okay."

Jackie reached for a towel, and somehow the bath mat

whizzed out from under her feet. She caught hold of a towel rack as she started to go down, and with a sharp crack it came off the wall; she slammed to the cold tiles with the chrome bar still in her hand. Then she was lying there with her head next to the toilet and Stu standing in the doorway.

"Jesus Christ," he said. "Are you all right?"

Jackie grabbed on to the side of the sink and pulled herself up. "Yeah," she said. "I don't know how that happened." One side of her body felt like it had been beaten with a club.

Stu took her arm, saying, "You oughta watch it, Jack." He led her over to the bed and she lay down. Stu tugged off his sweater, unzipped his pants, and dropped them onto the carpet. She felt the bruises begin to rise along her rib cage. Then they lay there together in the dark, her arm across his shoulder, and the wind sounding as if it came from a long way off. "We're out on the prairie," she whispered.

"Sure are," whispered Stu.

They came together very slowly, very warm under the thin blankets, and afterward, both fell asleep thinking about Randall Harper out on that porch.

When an incredibly bright light cut into the room, Jackie woke up and Stu wasn't there. She threw off the blankets—the cold air made her skin shrink on her arms. Her body ached.

She heard the engine of the sportscar and walked to

the window that overlooked the parking lot. A thick layer
of snow had fallen overnight. Jackie watched Stu moving
around the rumbling car, in and out of the pale cloud
rising from the exhaust, clearing the windows. Behind
him, the lot blended invisibly into fields running far away,
unbroken except for low fences and small trees heavy
with snow. In the foreground of this picture he was
moving, with his long graceful sweeps at the windshield,
the only life in all that white. Watching, she flinched at
the thought of how she admired him and how she had hurt
him. She saw him straighten and stare up at her, or at the
glare in the window, the ice scraper dangling from one
hand.

Jackie got dressed, and when Stu came back up to the
room she told him, "I don't deserve someone as good as
you. I don't want anybody else." He looked at her, then
came over and kissed her. "You know how I feel," he
said. His face was cold. For a moment, he held her
tightly, his cheek against her hair. "You shouldn't stand
in the window naked."

"You're right," said Jackie.

He stepped back and squeezed her hand. "I'm going
to pay."

"I'll meet you at the car," Jackie said. Stu left, and
she bunched their clothes into the bags and carried them
down to the car. The first time she'd laid eyes on Stu,
he'd been sitting there with Randall Harper, the engine
idling loudly, just as it was now, in front of Dom's
Donuts. Jackie had been wearing a stretch top, the fashion

back then, a pale blue one. Randall had stuck his head out
the window and yelled, "Sweetheart, my friend here
thinks you're mighty fine. What cup size you packing?"
Jackie always blushed at this memory. She wondered if
she'd see Randall again; most probably she would, during
Christmas visits.

She went back up to the room and checked under the
beds and in the bathroom, where two little holes marked
the place where the towel rack should have been. She
looked in the mirror, smiled at herself to check her teeth
for whiteness, then straightened her coat collar so that it
lay flat in back.

She picked up the last of their things, closed the door
behind her, pulled on her mittens, and walked back down
to the car. As she stepped off the snowy curb, the lot
vanished. Jackie's feet never touched ground. They
soared into the air and she was flung down onto the snow.
She landed halfway on and halfway off the curb.

Jackie's purse was open and its contents were scattered around her head like thoughts she was having. She
lay there, feeling the snow on her neck, looking up at the
bright sky, and she had to admit it: this pattern of events
was not normal, not at all normal.

She was wondering about this, almost feeling com-
fortable on her lumpy snow-bed, when a man came out
of a room nearby. He zipped a green army jacket and
squinted up at the sky. Jackie saw this upside down.

He came over and looked at her. "Do you need some

help, miss?'' He knelt down. He wore a nubby brown scarf and had a beard.

"Sure," she said. He helped her up, brushing a little of the snow off her back in what Jackie thought was a gentlemanly way, and started picking up a few of the lipsticks and pens that dotted the ground. He was a youngish man, and unusually polite. "Treacherous stuff, the snow. Real easy to slip," he said. "Gotta watch it. You did all right, though. Picked yourself right back up. That's the way."

Jackie smiled at him. Every bone and muscle from her neck to her knees seemed to hurt with a different pain.

The man handed her the snowy items from her purse. "Where are you headed?" he said, glancing at the idling car and back at Jackie.

She dropped a pen from her thickly mittened hands. He bent to pick it up. Jackie liked his curly reddish hair, cut short in back. "I'm moving," she said as he straightened up.

"Hey!" He grinned. "Moving house? To around here?"

Before she could answer, Stu came toward them on the walkway. Jackie watched Stu as he looked at the mark she'd made in the snow, at the man, at the damp smears on her coat. "You fell?" he said.

"Came out of my room and found her flat out," said the man. "She's okay, though." He stretched out his hand to Stu. "Bud Ficker. Glad to know you."

"Stu Dell." He looked at Jackie, and she knew he was wondering why this man was telling them his name.

"I really appreciate your help, Bud," said Jackie.

"Not at all," he said, smiling. Stu and Jackie gathered up their belongings and got into the car. As they backed out, the front end skidded a bit. They nearly hit Bud Ficker as he scraped the snow off his hatchback.

They pulled out onto the road, and the clearness of the morning was almost shocking. The light was brilliant, making their eyes narrow, making shapes seem to change as their car moved down the road. The sky was a clean blue pane; everything else was white and bright and chrome-edged, and everywhere the light bounced. Jackie felt as if she could see its path, from that patch of ice to that streetlight to the trim of their car.

They streamed along the wet roads, making fast gains, pushing into a new page of the highway atlas. It was the next day of the year. Jackie squinted out at the blinding countryside and thought: I'll try hard to be good.

She flipped down the sun visor. She brushed some dust off the mirror with her sleeve and ran her hand through the waves of her hair. "Well, we're still learning a lot," she said. "Still pretty young, right?"

She pushed the sun visor up, reached over, and gently stroked Stu's hair back off his face. "Not getting any younger," said Stu. His green eyes, the green of wet grass, didn't budge from the road ahead.

"I think you're the best," she said.

"When we get there," he said, "I'll drive right into the Pacific."

She gazed at him. He looked relaxed, pleased with himself. She turned to the window and wondered: was he driving with care? It might be easy to slip off the road. She weighed this possibility, wiggling her cold toes, and outside, the farms went flashing, skating, skimming by.

AVOIDING
DARLA

There wasn't any logic to Apres Jour. Little girls' leotards hung next to satin nighties on jammed racks. Panty-hose stalactites and fancy garters dangled from the ceiling. Sequined iron-on patches glittered in a glass case.

High upon a ladder, a young woman in a kimono pulled boxes from the shelves and peered into them. A little hunched-shouldered lady stood at the ladder's foot. "The one I want's got the side stretch panels shaped like lemons," she was saying as I walked in.

"Swear my heart, I'll find your fit, dear," said the younger one from her perch, smiling down on her customer.

That was my first picture of Darla. I remember her voice sounding way too musical for White Hill.

I've been in White Hill, Ohio, for two weeks now. I've been avoiding Darla for one. How long can you go, in a small town like this one, without accidentally bumping into somebody at the supermarket? Darla lives on a shady street near where the Ohio Central line crosses Merry Avenue. Once, a ketchup factory stood there on Merry, pumping out four hundred thousand gallons a year, and the smell was so strong some people still call that neighborhood Vinegar Town. But I myself think of it as Darlaland, and I've been steering clear.

The manager of the supermarket told me about that long-gone factory. He's who happened to pick me up, walking half-naked along the tracks by Merry Avenue, close to dawn last Friday. Since then, he's stopped by twice to check up on me. The poor guy is so bashful he can hardly look me in the eye, but I'm glad he comes. I'm more alone now than I ever have been.

This all began on a Friday evening, on my second night in White Hill. I was sitting by the window, listening to the radio, watching a rabbit graze the remains of my uncle's backyard garden, when the microwave of the Ferdinands, who rent the basement, threw some kind of radioactive fit. Down in their apartment, rugs, curtains, coats in the closet, all began to smoke. Dark clouds burst from the upholstery and were sucked upward into the main house. Sheets of smoke seeped in between the old floorboards, billowing in rows like black banners.

Unfortunately, I'd just done my hand washables and, for modesty's sake, had hung them to dry inside, all over the living room and dining room and sloping kitchen. All

my stuff was invaded by a fierce odor, plastic and sicken-
ing. It got into the fibers and wouldn't let go.

Gone in a noxious puff was my impressive collection
of lingerie—shell colors, jungle colors, midnight blue—
all bought for Gene. "I love you feeling slippery, Amy,"
he'd said once when we were in bed together back in the
apartment on East Capitol Street, D.C. We listened to
the radios hanging out one block over in front of the
China Quick, and Gene slid his hands across me. I wore
a rhubarb-colored camisole and matching tap pants, with
the scalloped edges and everything. That was my first real
lingerie, as opposed to just a nice bra or panties.

In the era of Eugene, which I suppose I can now tally
up—it lasted a year and eight months—I must have
bought a new underthing every other week. "I like it
when they smell new," he'd say, nuzzling my abdomen,
"like they're still on the hanger in Intimate Apparel." I
loved that smell, too.

That is how I ended up going to Apres Jour and meeting
Darla. In the White Hill directory, Apres Jour was the
only listed source for "Undergarments, Women."

I set out early the next morning, pearly sunshine
falling onto First Avenue. I walked past the fire station;
the men were polishing a truck, joking and laughing.
Their easy way with one another made me feel lonely. I'd
hardly spoken to a soul since I'd pulled into town three
days before.

In fact, not counting the panicky few moments with

the Ferdinands, the closest I'd come to human contact was a letter Gene had sent by overnight mail. "Please let's try again," he'd scrawled. "I love you, Amy, you love me. I feel myself changing all the time."

I'd been changing, too. I saw it in the dressing room mirror at Apres Jour. Gone was that honed edge I had back when I was wildly in love with Gene, the hungry look. Now there was a pinch extra on my hips; my hair had grown out, wispy light waves tucked behind my ears. When I tried on a slip with little lace hearts appliquéd across the chest, I thought, "Hell, why am I still buying this sexy junk?" I decided to check out something cheaper and more serviceable. But just then, Darla drew the curtain aside. She murmured, "You look like an angel in that. It makes your shoulders look rosy."

As she rang up the slip and some sensible underpants, Darla asked me where I was from. The store was deserted, and we talked as she straightened the evening bags in the glass case between us. I told her about my dead uncle Jim's house, how when I moved out on Gene, my mom said, "Go sort out your uncle's worldly goods, take a summer for yourself."

"That house might be on the market a long time," Darla said. "There isn't a whole lot of influx around here." She smiled. "It'd be nice to have you in town awhile." She told me how the Ku Klux Klan ran all the gas stations, and I should remember to lock my doors because the town wasn't as safe as it seemed. "They can fence those hi-fis fast in Toledo,'' she said. ''So fast you wouldn't believe.''

She got busy with a new customer then, and waving good-bye, I headed out onto First, wandering in and out of the few stores, looking for replacements for the scorched drapes. Shopping took my mind off the fact that I was swiftly running out of money. I'd been teaching geometry in a girls' junior high in D.C. Usually, I stayed through the summer session. Now I wasn't sure I wanted go back in the fall. My mother had said she'd send a little money to tide me over. When I got home from down-town, I found an envelope from her in the mailbox. On her thick stationery, in her bold hand, she'd written, ''Eugene came over and demanded to know where you were. Honey, I had to tell him. He was threatening to quit his job to go looking for you. All my love, Mom.'' No money.

The phone was ringing as I opened the screen door. I stopped. Retreating to the porch swing, I listened to it through the screen. It wheedled on and on, sounding angry and breathless. I pulled the new slip out of the bag and smoothed it across my lap. I wondered how things could so quickly turn so terrible between people. I wanted to cry.

I was, however, Gene-free by my own choosing—I knew that—and so I resisted tears. When the telephone finally fell silent, I went in and made myself a ham sandwich. The smell of smoke was strong, but it was bearable. I ate my sandwich sitting on the bedroom floor, contemplating my uncle's clothes as I munched. The phone began to ring again. I took it off the hook and stuffed the receiver between the mattress and the box spring. Then I started to sort through the suits and ties, making one pile for my brother and one pile for charity.

Lovers think they have rights. They think in terms of entitlements, obligations. Which is fitting, I guess, because your love is your only true property. The earth owns all the rest, and takes it back, eventually.

I took the receiver out from the bed and replaced it onto the cradle. This time, it remained silent.

Darla visited the next evening. "My dad and I used to always do a welcome wagon, dragging my little red wagon full of picture hooks and junk," she said, handing me a loaf of banana bread.

When I'd seen her tall form at the screen door, peering in with her face close to the mesh, I felt flush with relief, so happy it was a little embarrassing. I'd spent the afternoon paging through a list of teaching jobs, trying to imagine myself in Seattle or Atlanta. When I'd looked up from the booklet, the heat and emptiness of my uncle's house seemed to vibrate. No sound came from the Ferdinands' apartment. They were retired farmhands, and I pictured them lying down there, limp, all their energy wrung out of them by hard living.

While I stirred up some ice tea and unwrapped

Darla's still-warm gift, she wandered into the living room. "The layout of my house is not all that different from this," she said. I heard her open the cabinet of the dusty-faced grandfather clock and wind it.

We cooled off, sitting on the porch. "I was thinking I might have met your uncle." Darla broke a slice of banana bread in half. Her nails were painted coral-color. "Did he work at the bank?"

I nodded, taking a slice for myself. "Parts of my family founded that bank."

"Oh?" Darla chewed. "He was a good-looking old guy."

"I wasn't very close to him." I said. "My mom wasn't speaking to him most of the time I was growing up."

"Why do people hold grudges?" Darla said, shaking her hair back from her face. She gazed at her hands, wrapped around her wet ice-tea glass. "My husband wants me to get pregnant." She looked up at me. "I said forget it—I'm too young and having too much fun. Right?"

"Right." I wondered how old Darla was. I guessed she was close to my age—twenty-eight. I was pregnant last year, and Gene had assured me that only my vote counted.

"Men will think it's so easy. It's fun for them," Darla said.

"I want to have kids when the time's right."

"I wonder about it. I think people have kids because

they think it'll make them live forever." Darla swirled
the ice in the bottom of her glass. "But, Jesus, they give
you a lot of grief and you go ahead and die anyway."

A car nosed into the driveway next door, and a man
with a metal tool kit climbed out. Darla stood and walked
to the edge of the porch. "Hey, Ronnie," she called to
him.

"How's it going, Darla?" he said, scowling shyly. He
nodded at me, looking a little confused, and disappeared
into his garage.

"We had our high school lockers next to each
other," Darla said. "Monahan. Moore."

"So you're . . . what? Monahan?"

She smoothed her painted thumbnail across her upper
lip, a gesture that I came to see as her tic. "Used to be
Moore," she said.

Apres Jour is closed on Mondays. Darla had me over for
a professional manicure, a skill she said she learned from
her sister, who owned a beauty shop in Detroit. That
night, I wrote to my mother: "I've made a friend. She's
grown up here in this town and never left it, so different
from us, moving around everywhere. She's fascinating—
knows some things about life. I admire that."

She led me through her living room, where dead
flowers hung upside down, clipped to wire skirt hangers
and hooked on the backs of chairs. "This is my latest
thing, flower drying." She sighed. "Not a whole lot of
choices around here."

In the den, a midday news program played with the
sound off. A low coffee table in front of a corduroy couch
had been set with bottles of polish, tissues, hand lotion.
We sat, and she picked up one of my hands. "So small,"
she murmured, turning it, patting it all over, like fruit she
might be buying. She looked up at me. "I think you've
got to go for a straight-out red. With your coloring and
everything."

I smiled and shrugged. "Sure, I'm on vacation."

As she began filing, she glanced up at the television,
a clip of soldiers drilling, somewhere in South America.
"We can turn the sound up if you want. This is the way
I watch lately. I want to keep up, but the news has been
so bad."

"This is fine." I was enjoying being tended to, the
soft tickle at the ends of my fingertips.

"I always wanted to move out, to a New York or a
Washington, but I have to admit it, I think I was just
scared." Her brown hair slid across her cheekbone as she
bent over my hand.

"You don't seem like you'd scare easily."

She looked up, rolled her eyes. "I know, I know."
She shook her head and held my fingertips up to her lips,
blew the dusty filings away with warm damp breath. She
let out a small laugh. "That's the way I come off, anyhow."

Through the door to the kitchen, I could see a pair of
men's running shoes, tongues hanging out, laces in knots,
tucked under a chair. "Is your husband home?"

"Doing business with his brother in Chicago. Don't talk about him to me."

"Okay."

She kneaded lotion into my hands. "We're not getting along these days." She picked up the squat bottle of polish and shook it furiously, the little ball clattering within. "Don't get married."

"Don't worry," I said. "I'm not even close."

She held out her hand, palm up, and I rested mine across it, my fingers stiff, expectant. She touched the cool brush to the middle nail and drew it down, very slowly.

When Gene and I broke up, it was sudden, sharp—like the snapping of a major bone in your body, a femur. On June tenth, all was fine: we ate out, we had sex. The night of the eleventh, I was rolling out the sofa bed at Mom's.

What happened in between? I'd tugged on his hair in the near dark. I'd teased him, asking, "What about me would you change if you could?"

If he hadn't been in that smooth-brained post-love-making daze, he probably wouldn't have answered as easily as he did: "I'd make you taller and smarter."

I sat up. "Smarter?"

He curled away from me for a moment, pressed his hands to his face, muttered, "Oh no," and then rolled back, trying to get his arms around my waist. But I struggled free. "Listen," he said.

"Why smarter? Why would you think that?"

"You are smart," he groaned, sitting up. "Just sometimes I wonder if you understand certain things I say. That's all I mean."

I swung my legs over the edge of the bed. "I don't care about most of what you say." And at that moment, this struck me as the truth.

"Why are we even talking about this? What do you expect when you ask someone a question like that—'What would you change about me?' " He threw the sheets off his legs. I moved around the bare-floored room, our pile of clothes, a shelf of books, feeling like I'd found a crack in our love, and was peering into it, like the man in New Mexico who walked past an ordinary rock and felt a kind of wind coming from it. He came back with a shovel and a pick and learned he'd been walking above a dark deep void. I dawdled around the room, touching the bookshelf, the edge of the desk. The small of my back prickled. "I don't think I love you," I said.

I looked over my shoulder at Gene, crouched in the twisted sheets. I saw the dark sockets of his eyes, the soft line of his jaw, and I knew it could very well be true. "I don't love you," I said.

The next night, my mother said, "*Of course* you're smart," as she plucked cushions from the fold-out couch and stacked them on the carpet. "You scored well on all your tests, you're a teacher." I stood by my suitcase, an old blue nightgown and my toothbrush in hand. She came over, gathered me in her arms, and gave me a hug. "You write poetry," she said, her voice warm in my ear. "Your brother Dave never writes poetry."

. . .

Tuesday afternoon was gasping hot. The phone had been ringing again, all day long, and I couldn't bring myself to answer. Instead, I lugged a heavy wooden porch chair down to a patch of shade cast by the high yew bushes in the front yard. I settled down with a mystery from my uncle's shelf of yellowing paperbacks.

Around five o'clock, an old station wagon, flat and long as a barge, made its way up the street and stopped in front of my house. All the windows were down and Darla sat inside, apparently naked. I stood up and crossed the lawn to her.

"I'm going for a swim. Join me?" She was wearing a small yellow bikini. Her stomach was pale and a bit folded, like pastry dough. She smiled at me and raised her brows questioningly.

She sat at the kitchen table while I changed into my suit, an aqua one-piece bought years ago for a trip to Puerto Rico with a boyfriend I could barely remember. I heard her leafing through a pile of bills I had stacked there. "Electricity is expensive in this town, isn't it?" she called to me, then laughed. "I guess we should be thankful we've got it at all."

"I'm starting to think I like it here," I called from the bedroom.

"Yeah," Darla said. "Talk to me in thirty-one years."

I threw on one of my uncle's shirts as a cover-up. I'd

never paraded around in a suit like Darla was doing. I'd
have felt unprotected, somehow. But when we walked
out the kitchen door and around to her car, she held her
long body easily, her white back gleaming, glazed by the
sun. Her stride was smooth and loose. I walked behind
her, impressed.

We drove through the fields west of town, lined with
late-June weeds; redwing blackbirds perched on the wire
fences. They made me think of my uncle Jim. When he
came for his one and only visit, we lived in Binghamton,
New York. He was dismayed by the crows that squabbled
in the dirty park across from our house. "At home we've
got nicer ones," he told me as we walked. "Smaller and
quieter, with the neatest little patch of red on each
wing." I must have been eight or nine; he held my
mittened hand in his. It is my only memory of him.

We rose over a hill planted with soy, and there was
Lake Marvin, wide and dark, framed by forest. Small
boats dashed through its blue-black center, curved around
a peninsula, and disappeared. The road dipped down and
into the woods. Darla said, "I am so excited. This is the
prettiest spot in the county." She smiled over at me.
"How long's it been since you've been swimming?"

"I couldn't tell you."

"It's something you ought to do, just so you remember you can float. I used to come out here all the time."

The sun was strong and warm. It slanted over the tops
of the trees on the far shore and polished the calm surface.

Darla had brought a blow-up raft, and as she stood ankle-deep in the water puffing air into it, I shrugged off my shirt and slipped quickly into the lake, turned, and collapsed backward into the water. It flowed up to my neck, cool as satin, a fresh green-blue. I swirled in it, closing my eyes. I wanted to forget my lonely worries, the fretting phone.

A moment later, Darla was circling me, the water moving from her kicks. She clasped the faded red raft under her, her upper body angling out of the water. Her shoulder blades stuck out sharply, channeling her wet hair between them.

I paddled toward her and stretched my arms across the empty half of the raft. She stopped kicking and we drifted, heads resting on the warm, rubber-smelling surface, hips just touching as our legs dangled out behind us. "Thanks so much, Darla," I sighed after a moment. "This is just the thing."

"Yeah." She smiled.

The water, trees, sky, boats, flickered gold and blue, in and out of existence. My ear pressed to the raft, I could hear the air inside it. I imagined I was adrift at sea, alone, but safe, warm, and free from care. A thought came, like a parachute opening: I am very young. . . . How much time there is in my life. Somehow, out on the water, I could see more possibility.

I was facing away from Darla when I felt her hand on my head. "Your blond goes away when it's wet."

"It's my roots showing through." I lifted my head and she took her hand away. I turned toward her and rested my cheek on the raft. Her eyes were close, dark, and shiny as oil.

She brushed a strand of wet hair from her mouth—the movement was theatrically slow, languid—with her lacquered nails. She brought her hand to her lips, kissed her palm softly, and laid it across my face.

I shut my eyes. I was frozen, heart stilled, under the weight of her hand. For an instant, I lay submerged, with the raft beneath me: I was down, down in the silken murk of the lake bed.

Then I felt a kiss, soft as water, brush my lips. Her movement on the raft made a fresh flush of water run up under my chest and chin. I lay with my eyes closed a long minute, unsure if it had happened, if it would happen again; it didn't.

I opened my eyes and looked at Darla. Her face was serious and expectant. She was very close. Faint, tiny freckles were sprinkled on either side of her nose. She looked beautiful.

She moved her hand over mine where it rested on the raft. Every inch of my skin felt stretched thin. The whole world was expanding, doubling in size, and it made me light-headed. I think I grinned at her. Behind her, the lake water stretched to the horizon.

A motor bawled so loudly we both lifted our heads, and a small boat holding a man and three children in life jackets whizzed by close. One little boy, using both hands, held up a line to show us a huge dangling catfish. Darla waved at him.

We swam back to the shallows, and a shyness overcame me. I walked uncertainly in my bare feet up the rock-strewn shore to the grass. My skin tingled as the sun dried the droplets from my back. On the little spit of land where we'd parked, a young couple and their children had made a nest of bright plastic toys and picnic things under a tree. Darla spread her towel on the grass and I sat on one corner. I took a comb from my purse and began to work intently at untangling the snarls of my hair. Darla lay back in the weakening light and sighed.

I spent a long time freeing my hair from knots, struggling to think about what had happened. But I didn't have much success. My mind kept fogging. It was like when I used to smoke joints before teaching and then had to fight to remember where I was in the lesson.

Eventually, the picnicking family packed up its things. Their car crunched on the gravel and was gone. In the evening light, Darla pulled on my arm, and I lay down next to her. Her hair across my face was cool and rich, and her skin was soft from the water.

Some things happen and it seems like the whole world is in on it. Not people, necessarily, but the actual forces of the world—gravity, time, things like that—conspire to provide the opportunity. That's what happened with Darla and me. Ordinarily, we may not have been much

more than friendly faces to each other, people who might
stop for a cup of coffee if we met on the street. But the
world turned its glance our way, and our lives collided.

We drove home in near silence. I watched the bugs
and moths in the headlights and struggled to get my
bearings, to come up with a plan. When we pulled up in
front of Uncle Jim's, Darla said, "Oh look, you got
flowers." The yellow bulb over the porch steps dropped
light onto a cluster of roses stuck in a green glass vase and
wrapped in cellophane.

Alarmed, I glanced at Darla, and she lowered her
eyes, as if she didn't want to seem nosy. "Somebody's in
demand," she said. A smile lifted one corner of her
mouth.

"Yeah, but can I handle it?" I said, my throat suddenly sore.

"Sure you can," she said. "I'll see you tomorrow or
the next day."

"Great," I croaked, stumbling out of the car.

I felt short of breath as I read the little card edged in
pink foil. "Please call me at the Blue Top Motel when
you get in. I've driven fourteen hours. Backups due to
construction on Pa. turnpike. Love you, Gene." His
handwriting was sloppier than usual.

I carried the flowers inside and set them down in the
entryway, swerved into the bedroom to pull on jeans and
sandals, strode through the kitchen and out the back
door. Above the yard, the stars seemed blurred; through
the damp grass I charged, stumbling like the ground was

tilting, the earth was revving up its speed. The Blue Top
sat two blocks away through backyards. I plunged past
swing sets and mulberry hedges, ducking under clothes-
lines. Warm windows of light and voices sailed by, and
then, breathing hard, I emerged onto Linden, with the
Blue Top low and tidy-looking across the way.

Gene's car was one of only three in the lot. The motel
office flickered with television light. He was in there,
shifting uncomfortably in a folding chair. A chubby teenage girl with blond bangs lounged in a recliner, a cigarette
in her many-ringed hand. They both stared at a loudly
playing set.

I marched into the office. Gene jumped up, his hands
rising toward me. "Amy," he said with a delighted smile.
His curly hair had been cut recently and badly, and he
looked exhausted.

"This is not good, Gene," I said, backing away as he
rounded the counter. "I'm sorry you came all this way."

"Listen. Okay? Please listen to me." He stopped his
approach, bit his lip, and picked up a ceramic poodle
from the counter, turning it nervously in his hands.

"Amy, do you really mean to break up a good relationship because of one conversation? Is that sensible?"
He looked at me and added quickly, "Not that I don't
think you're sensible—I do, I truly do. But couldn't we
talk about this? I mean—" he began to say; then, glancing
at the girl, he lowered his voice and returned the poodle
to its post. "Couldn't we talk about this outside? At the
house, maybe?"

"No," I said. His weary tone scraped my heart, and
I remembered, in bruising flashes, several things I loved
about him: his gallantry, his wonderful family, his ease
with kids. Then I noticed he was gawking at my burning-
cherry fingernails. I curled my hands into fists, embarrassed. He stared at me.

"I want you to come back to Washington," he said.
The girl rose from the chair to change the channel on the
set. The leathery chair squeaked as she flopped back into
it. "Look." Gene was almost whispering now, leaning
toward me. "If I promise to leave here—right now—will
you promise to think about it?"

I leaned against the wall and shook my head.

"Amy, I've been saving up for an engagement ring for
months," he said softly. My knees felt as if they might
give way. I took a deep breath and glanced over at the
girl. She puffed her cigarette, regarding me speculatively.

"If you leave," I said, "I'll think about it. But that's
all I can promise."

"Okay. That's all I want. I'm going to get back in the
car right now."

"You're gonna lose your deposit," said the girl.

As we crossed the parking lot, he took my hand. The
air was muggy and still; crickets droned in dark woods
beyond the motel's blue-shingled mansard. I glanced up
at the sky, the stars, and noticed a soft half-moon tilting
just above the treetops.

Gene said, "I've been watering your plants." Startled
by his voice, and with my hand resting in his, I realized

my mind had conjured Darla there beside me. Looking at him, I felt a hot blush rise in my face; I yanked my hand from his. He opened the car door, frowning. "You ought to get some sleep," I suggested, feeling guilty. "You could stop in Toledo."

"Maybe I will." He slid into the car, staring ahead as he started the ignition. He looked up at me with a grim little smile. I knew he felt his trip was a failure. "Call me?" he said.

I nodded tightly, avoiding his eyes. "In a little while."

Before his car had cleared the parking lot, my mind was already across town. I headed east, past the auto-parts store. Inside the chain link fence of Flore's Garden Center, a small crowd of stone ducks and elves glowed at me, knowing looks in their big smirky eyes. I pleaded with them as I passed. Am I actually walking to this woman's house?

No, the elves cried. Turn right at Johnson Street, go get a sundae at the Dairy Queen. Good idea, I told them. Excellent idea.

But I ate a strawberry sundae, my mouth felt sticky and I still couldn't steer myself home. The milkweeds were tossing in the vacant lot I passed on my way down Second Street. A breezy front swept into town. Feathery seed floated above the field, glittering. The air blew warm and wheat-smelling through my hair. My feet steered me northerly.

Lights were on and machinery rattled in the lumber-yard; people piled laughing out of a bar on Milo Street; and then I cut across a concrete plot all glowing pale, traced with cracks like a freezing lake. Wires stuck straight out of the cement in clusters like headless field daisies. The town dropped away here, and all of Ohio opened out around me, and the universe flew off into infinity above. I stopped, put my hands to my mouth. Where am I? I am far, far from everywhere, in the middle of nowhere; I am becoming unmoored. I am drifting dangerously.

I started walking again. I'm tired, I said aloud. I'm going home. But I crossed Merry Avenue and turned into Darla's street.

One soft light glowed in an upstairs window. I could see Darla. She was wearing a green tank top; she read a small, leather-bound book, maybe a Bible or a diary, or poetry. Gold light flowed down her hair.

The door swung open.

"I was in the neighborhood," I said.

"What a surprise." She smiled.

Wednesday morning early, I stumbled back to Uncle Jim's and slept straight through the day, then sat awake all that hot Wednesday night, more frightened than I've ever been. I wondered where this encounter with Darla was headed. Where was I headed? On Thursday after-noon, the money from my mother was waiting in the mailbox when I surfaced from a drowned sleep at two.

Trying to clear my head, I forced myself to work, putting Jim's *National Geographics* into cartoons, sorting through his collection of foreign bills and coins. In the evening, I went out for packing tape and milk.

But next to the Supersave was a little dress shop, and in the window, on a sprightly headless mannequin, was a one-piece strapless sunsuit, crimson to match my blazing nails. I'd never worn anything like it—it looked like something Darla would wear. I slipped inside and tried it on. "I'll wear it right now," I said, handing over the dress I'd had on. "Oh, good," said the saleslady. "It really looks adorable."

The new red sunsuit gave me the excuse, and the courage, to drop by Apres Jour. Inside the lighted shop, a fat elderly lady with sugar-white hair sat behind the counter eating a pear. I strolled in and asked for Darla. "She got me to watch the shop for her today, had an appointment up in Toledo." She smiled apologetically.

I drove down to her house anyway. The old station wagon was parked in the driveway, but the house looked completely still.

Darla answered my knock quickly. Her "hello" was so sharp, I thought my heart would crack. Her hand was tense, holding the door open. "You know I'm really happy you're here," she said with unmistakable dismay. I tugged up the top of my silly new purchase.

Her hair was pulled back in a braid and she wasn't wearing any makeup. It's amazing what a flick of mascara will do: without it, her eyes were small and set close on

either side of her nose. Her purse was slung over her
shoulder. "Oh—you were about to leave?" I stam-
mered.

"Just getting ready to drive out to my folks' place.
Why don't you come?"

"No, I can't—"

"Amy, please come," she said firmly. "I want you
to."

We drove along the road out of town. Darla's hands
rested on the wheel, her arms thin and graceful, and as
I looked at them, I felt my face go warm; I turned toward
the window, grateful for the darkness rolling down the
horizon. "I used to want to live on a farm," I said.
"When I was a kid."

She shrugged. "You'd hate it, probably. Lot of flies."
Her dismissive tone stung. The tires crunched over the
gravel-patched pavement. My mind offered up only inap-
propriate phrases, questions to ask.

"Well," she finally said, softly. "Funny news. Funny
because we were only just talking about it. Turns out I'm
pregnant."

I came up blank. Maybe I'd heard her wrong.
"What?"

"Yeah." She looked over at me. "I just found out this
afternoon."

I met her eyes. She seemed to read my thoughts.

"I think I did know earlier, in some way," she said
carefully. "I knew it might be a possibility, anyway. And
I guess I was shying from the idea, a bit."

"And now you're not?"

"No." She gazed down the road. "I'm accepting my fate."

A note of excitement betrayed her. Her acceptance was already giving way to joy. The world coasted away from me then. Darla talked softly, something about her folks, they'd wanted this so long. Her voice shook, we were rattling over a cattle guard. She mentioned her husband. We drew up to a gateless railroad crossing. Three lights winked.

I felt I was plummeting; far below lay that meadow of concrete with its crop of dead wire. I needed to grab hold of something—anything—and so I turned to her. Just as my fingertips grazed her arm, she stepped on the brakes and blurted, "I don't feel good about what happened. Do you?" She pressed her lips tight together and looked at me. "I don't think it was right." Then the car was flooded, yellow as morning light, and I saw her eyes were half-shut, glittering with tears. "I'd like to forget about it."

"Darla," I whispered. My fingers, where they'd touched her, felt burned. I jerked the door handle and half fell, half leapt from the car. I needed air. The wind was warm on my bare shoulders. I took a few steps, let the car door swing shut. Stumbling down the embankment, I reached a pitch-black ditch and hopped across, weeds brushing my legs. Darla called after me. I scrambled up the other side and into a field of something high and ticklish.

Darla had gotten out and stood looking in my direc-

tion. Over the din of the approaching train, I could hear
her. "Amy, where are you going? Christ, Amy, wait a
second!"

I turned back toward the station wagon. Out beyond
it, the train was growing closer. Darla looked over her
shoulder at it, then back toward me. Her hair was flicking
around her face; I could just barely see it in the strange
light.

"Amy!" Her voice was rising to a screech. "Come
on!"

She stared out at me. "Please! That's a half-hour
train!"

"Just leave!" I cried, as loudly as I could. But I wasn't
sure if she heard me, for the train was now thunderous.
Darla looked back at it, only one small field away, then
out toward me one more time. She hesitated for an
instant longer, then hurried around the car and slid in,
pulling the door closed behind her. The car shot forward
and bumped over the tracks, disappearing down the in-
cline on the far side.

I drew a long, shaky breath. The train barreled
through the crossing.

I try to imagine what it would have been like if, groggily
steering my car home from an all-night euchre game, I'd
seen a woman with curly blond hair wandering along the
railroad tracks in a dirty strapless outfit.

Hal the supermarket man slowed down and kindly
inquired if I needed a lift.

He shook his head and said, ''That's a ways,'' when
he heard where I'd walked from, said I must have come
five miles. He was too polite or shy to ask why I'd been
wandering out there, or how long. Eight, nine hours, I
guess it was, but I didn't walk it straight through; I
stopped to sleep for a while in some high soft grass.

I slept many more hours when I finally got back to the
house that morning. Hal stopped by the same evening,
mumbling apologetically about being concerned. I made
him some coffee. I asked him if he knew Darla.

He took a long noisy sip from the white mug. Then
he nodded, a lock of silver hair falling down over his
forehead. ''Sure. Webb Simmons's wife. Pretty girl,'' he
said.

How long can I go in this town, avoiding Darla? It's been
a week already. I could just pack up and leave, go back,
maybe talk things through with Gene. But I need to stay
here for now, awkward as that might be. I've got to give
certain events a hard look and decide how they might fit
into a lifetime.

Tonight I went to the White Hill Lounge with old
Hal. I watched the door. She didn't come through it.

Driving me home, Hal gunned the car over the tracks
while a train was bearing down, not more than fifty yards
away. Death by train is relatively painless, he said, and
better than waiting all night, counting cars.

I'm not that way.

I stood there in the weeds in my ridiculous sunsuit

and counted each and every passing car. Finally the last one flew by, crowned by red lights. I could still feel the weight of Darla's forehead resting on my shoulder. I stayed to watch after that train, even, before I started back toward town.

PAYABLES

Rita's station wagon swerves into the driveway a little too fast. The grocery bag next to her topples, and taco fixings—a head of iceberg, a box of shells, Tabasco—slide out across the seat. Driving up, Rita has been staring at the front stoop of her unit, where a girl is seated nose-to-knees like an airline passenger waiting to crash. As the car comes to a halt, the girl lifts her head. Rita sees that Violet Burke, who lives around the corner, is weeping. The curves of her cheeks are slick in the sunlight.

Rita sits there for a moment with her hands on the wheel, worried. Then, leaning over, she gathers up the groceries lodged in the gap between the far end of the seat and the door and wonders how to greet the crying girl. She tries to imagine where her son might be on this breezeless afternoon.

She opens the car door and steps carefully onto white

high heels. Too high. She has worn them on account of
a luncheon honoring a mob of travel agents from the
Great Lakes states. Rita works for the chamber of commerce in Lauderdale. Heading up the walk, she wishes
only to withdraw into her house and escape from her
shoes. It is four o'clock, and smaller children on the block
are playing with skates and skateboards. They scream and
grind the wheels across the pavement.

Violet Burke is rubbing her face with the back of one
hand. Schoolbooks are stacked on the stoop next to her
hip. Rita looks at the bright slogan on the uppermost
book: *"¡Hablemos Español Hoy!"*

"Charlie's at the blacktop, shooting baskets," Violet
says.

"Is everything all right?" Rita says.

"Yeah." She stands up. Tears still flow down her
face. Rita, shifting the weight of the groceries to her hip,
feels a horrible radiation coming from Violet, hot teen
gloom and anger. Off in the empty field behind the row
of town houses, a dirt-bike engine sputters.

"There's nothing wrong?"

"Um, I don't feel free to talk about it with you,
ma'am." Violet picks up her books and holds them flat
against herself, against her sundress with its puckered top
and bright stripes squirming across and back. "Charlie
better watch it, I think."

"What?" says Rita, alarmed. "What do you mean?"

"You better ask him, not me."

The girl's grim face is set in parentheses of fine blond

hair. Her tiny nostrils and half-closed eyelids look bitten, a fiery red, and her lips glitter with strawberry lip gloss.

"Violet, you know how awful boys are. You know." Rita gives a little shrug and attempts an understanding smile. "Someone does a thing without meaning to, or says something or other."

Violet nods tightly. "I know." She stares for a moment at the red geraniums in pots along the side of the stoop. "Your flowers are really nice," she says. She turns and walks across the lawn toward the street.

Upstairs, Rita peers through the curtains of her bedroom window as she steps down from her heels and unbuttons her blouse. Violet has reached the end of the block and is just turning onto the cross street. She lives with her mother in a two-bedroom model. The lawns she passes are small and mostly dry yellow this June. No one here owns sprinklers.

Rita is mystified. She's scarcely seen Violet except standing at the high school bus stop. And she knows Violet's mother, Brenda Burke, only slightly—a woman with pineapple-yellow hair. Rita remembers introducing Dean to her at the school science fair. He'd watched as she walked off past a row of lockers toward the cafeteria. "Push-up bra and a girdle," Rita had whispered, tugging on his arm, pulling him in the opposite direction.

Slipping off her skirt, Rita stretches across the bed in her nylons and unbuttoned blouse, utterly worn out, battered by her day. Her stomach is pale and a little flabby above her waistband. She wants Dean to be there, humming to her, rubbing her shoulders, but he won't be home for hours. When he's not with her, time drags.

Last night they'd argued. Dean is running out of money. He had owned Cozy Car car-wash franchises, but in the time she has loved him, the car washes have gone under. They'd quarreled about his going to the track. Lately, their fights have been much more frequent, almost every other day. He'd said he'd been crunching numbers, talking to trainers. He'd said that meeting people around the track is crucial for getting a system down.

"That's pure nonsense," Rita had protested. "There is no system for horses. They've got their own wills. You can't predict what a living thing like that's going to do."

"Be a skeptic, okay, if that's what you want. That's fine." He ran a hand over his trim black hair; Dean is a former army man. He was sitting up in bed browsing through the racing form, circling names and numbers with red, blue, and green felt pens. "You live with a man for a year, and you can't grant him a bit of your faith." He didn't look at her. "If you ask me, that stinks."

"I've got plenty of faith," Rita said. "More than I know what to do with. That's the problem." She turned off the reading light on her side of the bed and rolled over to face the wall. Yes, he had questionable business judgment at times—but he deserved better than this, she fretted. He was a wonderful person.

"Christ, I'm hardly gonna throw money away. Not now. I mean, this is for you, Rita. I'm not getting married with fifty cents in my pocket. That's not the way I do things.'' He turned a page of the racing form, newsprint rustling. ''I want to look out for you and Charlie,'' he said quietly. She turned back toward him then, laid her head on his chest. As she'd pressed herself to him, her sorrow had ebbed away.

Now Rita pulls herself off the bed and drifts back to the window. A small boy is being jerked down the sidewalk by a sniffing dog. No sign of Violet Burke, no sign of Charlie. Tacos are his favorite; maybe they will draw him out of his fourteen-year-old's silence.

Rita slips on jeans and wanders down to the kitchen. She gets herself a beer and then empties the bag of groceries, setting the supper ingredients out on the counter. She slits the cellophane on a package of ground chuck and dumps it into a mixing bowl.

Charlie is off in the neighborhood, and Dean is at Hialeah. She hopes he is winning. Rita herself has been there only once, years ago. They took Charlie there, she and Jonathan. Not to the races but to the lagoons. More than two thousand varieties of fauna are protected in the gardens of Hialeah, including ''the world's only flock of flamingos that propagates in captivity,'' it said on an ad. They'd gone one weekend when Charlie was just starting first grade. He yelled at the famous flamingos, who calmly continued grazing in the black water, looking pink and wobbly. Rita can remember the colors of the striped T-shirt Charlie wore. She and Jonathan sat together on a bench and watched him turn somersaults.

She hasn't seen Jonathan in a long while. In the pictures Charlie showed her of their fishing trip last spring, he had less hair and more paunch than she'd remembered. And Charlie is so lanky; it seems incredible to Rita that he once curled himself up into such a tiny ball and rolled across the wet green grass. And now he is making teenage girls cry.

In a week, he'll be going to stay with Jonathan in Charleston. He'll be gone all summer.

To escape that thought, Rita busies herself browning the beef, then remembers, with a gasp, that she has yet to call the florist. As she flips through the phone book, she makes a wish that the shop is still open. A man answers. Heavy-metal music is roaring in the background. She orders a dozen white roses, gives the address twice because of the din. She recites the message for the card: "You are the love of my life. Always, Rita." It's a little embarrassing, saying this to a man on the phone. But it doesn't seem to faze him; he simply shouts, "Will do."

Dean is turning thirty-nine tomorrow. Rita herself has recently celebrated forty-two. She is sure that Dean, with his body sleek from sit-ups and his careless way of rising from a chair to shake a person's hand, will not look his age for a long time yet. This concerns Rita. She'd met Dean when he came to the chamber of commerce seeking marketing advice. At that time, Rita had been on four dates in the six years since her divorce. She wanted so much to marry again.

.　　.　　.

The town-house unit is on a rise about three miles from the ocean. The sunsets seem local, somehow. Rita sits in the kitchen at the table, a women's magazine spread out before her, pleased by the scene outside: hot yellow and pink in the sky, hot yellow and pink in the bougainvillea that run along the high wooden fence in back. She and Charlie moved to this place when he was nine. The fence reminded him of General Custer's stockade.

The front door opens, then shuts; she notices that he doesn't slam it anymore when he comes in. She wonders if Charlie's comings and goings are becoming stealthy. "Hello there," she calls.

"Hi," he says, appearing in the doorway. "Got a huge bruise on my thigh. Went for a slide right on top of a steak bone."

"What on earth?"

"Dog." He pulls out a chair, the legs squeaking against the linoleum. "Sometimes the fielders dive right into dog shit."

"Oh please," Rita says. Then a thought occurs to her. "You were supposed to be playing basketball."

"Nope." Charlie has brownish-red hair; he insists that it be long enough in front to cover his forehead, which he thinks is weird-looking. He has Rita's dark blue eyes and he's skinny. This bothers her every once in a while, and she urges egg-and-cream concoctions on him. Increasingly, however, her efforts strike her as fruitless, a losing battle she is waging against the energies inside him, forces, she imagines, that she might hear buzz and crackle if she were allowed to press her ear against his shirtfront.

The subject of Violet Burke looms in her mind as she puts dinner for Charlie and herself on the table. The girl was crying as if the world were at an end. Rita remembers her own tears, the variety of occasions and reasons: the humiliations of the divorce, her terror at growing old alone. Charlie has witnessed them all. He has switched on the little TV and tuned in a game show.

"Violet Burke was here today," she says, sitting down.

"Yeah?" Charlie is working intently on taco construction. "It's my business, right?"

"Yes."

He sips a glass of orange soda. "She's been on my nerves." He looks at Rita. He is not going to talk. Rita is, as she knew she would be, sorry she brought it up.

"The coach says I need hand weights." Music, bells, and fuzzy cheers erupt from the small speaker. Charlie stares at the screen.

Rita knows that there are few boys at school who bat better than Charlie, few who throw faster or harder. The words he uses when he jokes with his friends on the phone are truly filthy; they swim around in her ears. After overhearing his talk, she can't rid herself of it for hours.

There's a scab like a dash on his cheekbone. He'd come in with a bleeding cut and a half-believable story last Friday night. Looking at the mark, Rita feels a sharp thud in the area of her breastbone, as if some stranger, performing a resuscitative action, had stricken her there with the heel of his hand—this is her love for her son, nowadays.

"I'm not sure what's going on between the two of you," Rita says. She thinks she should tell him something about men and women. But then she balks. Her marriage to Jonathan seemed to end, after all, over his impatience with the seasickness she suffered whenever they went out on the boat he'd bought them. He'd accused her of showing no interest in his passions, no imagination. And now this craziness with Dean—what could she tell Charlie about love?

"You really ought to be nice," she says, smiling a little. "Girls' feelings are very easily hurt."

"Uh-huh," says Charlie. "I'm always nice to girls, Mom." He smirks at her and moves to get up from the table. "I'm nice to you, aren't I?"

"Some of the time," Rita says to his back as he bounds out of the room, and she decides to leave it at that.

The doorbell sounds, a short nasty buzz. When she opens the door, she finds the stoop deserted, the yard empty. The skating children and all others have gone inside. There is something stillborn and awful about their neighborhood at dusk, she thinks.

On the welcome mat sits a square envelope, drugstore stationery, printed with pastel rainbows. Rita picks it up; it's very thin, sealed, and marked "Charlie" in a neat penciled script. Rita returns to the kitchen and puts the note on the table. She traces the edges with her finger and stares out the back window. I'll be damned, she thinks, he's broken the girl's heart. Poor thing, she thinks. Poor girl.

A key turns in the front-door lock and Dean comes striding into the house, humming.

"Did you see Violet Burke lurking around out there?" Rita asks him, rushing into the living room.

"No, can't say I did, sweetheart." He meets her in midrush and kisses her mouth. Thoughts of Violet evaporate. He is wearing a red blazer that he swears is lucky. Rita thinks he might be mistaken for a movie usher in it, but she loves the way he looks anyhow. She is amazed that at any time or place, she can become starry-eyed just looking at him. She marvels at it still, after a year together. And he is such a good man.

"Well, well, well," he says, pulling her to him and running his hands down her back. "Ask me."

"How did you do?" says Rita.

"Hit the exacta, sweetheart. One-two-three."

"You're kidding. Wonderful!" Rita says, realizing nevertheless that it's no fabulous occasion when he wins. He doesn't have the cash to bet enough to win for real, to climb out of the hole he's in. She's not sure why he can't see this. "We'll have to celebrate."

Charlie comes barreling down the stairs. "Hey, Dean."

"Hiya, Charlie," Dean says, releasing Rita. "Get that

test back today?" They'd worked for hours last Sunday
night, the two of them, on algebra.

"Nope. Not yet." He plucks a pillow from the sofa
and drop-kicks it to Dean. Rita almost reprimands him,
but it's a threadbare old thing, and she loves the way
Dean and Charlie have been getting along lately.

She's back in the kitchen, piling Dean's dinner onto
a plate and listening to his and Charlie's voices, unable to
make out the words but appreciating Dean's smooth,
soothing low notes and Charlie's thinner, more urgent
timbre. Then she hears Dean say, "Jesus, Charlie," his
voice full of dismay. She freezes, her serving spoon hovering over the taco filling, and cocks her head toward the
door, straining to hear. But their voices have dropped to
tense murmurs. She sets Dean's plate onto the table.
When she steps into the living room, Dean looks up at her
with a frown and Charlie's glance darts to the floor. Her
son's cheeks are burning pink.

Rita feels something dangerous rumbling to life inside
of her. "What on earth—"

Dean cuts her off. "Chuck's got a little problem but
we're handling it, just the two of us." He smiles reassur-
ingly at her and nods, urging her silently to let him take
care of this.

Charlie is looking at her warily. She wants to pick him
up and shake him, but he's so large now—how heavy
he'd be. "A mysterious stranger left you a note," she
says, folding her arms tightly to her chest. She gestures

with her head toward the kitchen. He gets up, his hands thrust into his pockets, and steers clear around her.

She presses her hands to her mouth and closes her eyes, tired suddenly of the constant caretaking, tired of trying to hold things together. She feels as if she's reached the ragged edge of her personality, where the hem's coming undone. "Dean," she says, looking at him, taking a deep, shaky breath. "Please tell me if you are going to marry me or not." Suddenly the living room is too low; her neck feels bowed and cramped.

Dean looks at her, baffled, his brows traveling up the slope of his forehead. "Let's get a drink somewhere, okay?" he says.

Rita closes her eyes. "All right." She opens them, looking down at her flared jeans, a little tight across the hips. This is it, she thinks.

Dean drives a sportscar. In it, Rita always feels far from the rest of the world, peering out across the car's sweeping hood. Dean takes his hand off the gearshift and rests it over her knuckles. They drive out of the neighborhood of low, lighted houses guarded by aloes and palmettos, and turn onto the highway, passing a liquor store. In front, two boys rest their elbows on the roof of a car, cigarettes in their hands.

"So tell me what's going on with him," she says.

"Charlie is a rascal."

Rita thinks he is being kind. For the first time, she allows herself to consider real possibilities, real trouble.

But Charlie isn't hanging around with bad sorts. She'd read somewhere that a teen's friends are telling.

"This Violet offered to do it with him for twenty-five dollars." Dean looks at her. "That's what he said, 'do it with me.' "

"You aren't serious," murmurs Rita. Her small boy—she sees him turning somersaults.

He rolls down his window and sticks his arm straight out, palm outstretched for a moment. "So he did it with her, but of course he didn't have twenty-five bucks, so he says he just bolted, left her there."

Tears fill Rita's eyes, stinging tears. A hamburger joint and a carpet warehouse blur past like a movie out of focus. Dean squeezes her knee. "Rita."

"He's fourteen years old." Rita sniffs. "He's a monster." Regret rushes into her: she has left him alone too much; she has leaned on him too heavily in the years since the divorce. Maybe Jonathan should have had more time with him. "Turn around," she says. "Please turn around."

Dean shakes his head. "I promised him I wouldn't tell you, Rita. He believed me." He rubs his hand over his mouth. "This was our secret, okay?" He looks over at her. "Okay?" He turns and pulls up in front of a bar in an old house on the beach block. "Let's have that drink."

The place is run by a man named Richard, whom Rita knows from high school. In a corner, a young woman plays the piano and sings show tunes. The room is nearly empty—it is nine-thirty on a Tuesday night—and as

Dean guides Rita to a table in back, the woman is just winding up a rendition of "The Surrey with the Fringe on Top."

Rita watches Dean as he nods and smiles at Richard behind the bar, not understanding how he always summons up a hearty greeting for the world, but relieved that he does. She orders a martini, and Dean orders a whiskey sour. She stares at the table and tries not to think about the flatness in Charlie's eyes earlier that night, the girl's wet face in the afternoon light. Dean taps his fingers nervously, against the beat of the music. The drinks arrive, and Rita sips hers through the cocktail straw.

"Now listen to me," Dean says. He wraps his hands around his glass. "Today at the track, I made a substantial bundle of money." His voice is slow and heavy. He looks dead serious, his brown eyes working. "You hear me?"

"Yes."

"I found something out."

Rita plucks the straw from her glass and chews it. "Found out what."

"They drug the animals."

"You always hear that," she says. "Someone's always saying that."

"It's the truth," he says. Rita has an urge to plug her ears with her fingers and shut her eyes tight. She does not want to hear this.

"They give them drugs that numb them, to cut off the pain. I ran across a guy who sells the stuff, works at the zoo in Atlanta. Said they could be running themselves into the ground and they wouldn't know it." His dark brows draw together. "He gave me a good tip."

She snorts. "Great tip." Her mind conjures up flamingos picking timidly through the shallows on spindly legs. Dean leans forward, taking her hands in his. "It made me a bundle, Rita, and I want to put it to good use. Now we should get married."

"Married?" she says, her face hot now. "Married? That money is like stolen money."

"Don't be ridiculous."

"I can't help it." She needs air, she needs to get home to Charlie. She tries to pull her hands away, but Dean tightens his grip. His eyes are bright. "Nobody lost out on this." He says each word distinctly, each word its own sentence. "Nobody was hurt. Nobody."

"Violet Burke was hurt," Rita says. "What about her?"

"Rita, please." Dean looks at the table, frustration creasing his forehead, then back up at her. "I know what Charlie's done is painful for you. But he's a kid. And the girl will get her twenty-five."

"Oh, Dean," Rita whispers, yanking her hands from his grasp. She grabs her purse and hurries out of the bar.

The moon has come out, looking syrupy through the haze from the ocean. Rita comes to a stop at the car, parked where the street meets the beach. The breakers are faint white, rolling in. Rita pulls her sweater around her. And she realizes that she cannot face another five years alone. She cannot.

Dean comes up alongside her and puts his arm around her shoulder. Light angles from the door of a beachfront house next to the parking lot, and a woman's voice calls out, "Wolf! Come on. Wolf, get in here!" A small shaved dog tears past Dean's car and out into the darkness of the beach.

"Can we talk about this now?" Dean says.

"All right."

"I think we should do it right away. I've got the money. And Charlie's leaving."

"A week from Saturday."

"So there's no use waiting."

"I guess not." Rita wants so much to be married. She wants Dean. He opens the car door for her, and she climbs in. He is not perfect, but her desire for him is the clearest, deepest emotion she's felt since Charlie was an infant. He starts the ignition. She lets him take her hand and put it on the gearshift, then he rests his warm hand over hers.

"I love you, Rita," Dean says. "Why you've kept me around so far, I don't know, but now I plan to make it pay." He looks at her. "Beginning with this thing with Charlie. I'm going to handle it." He lifts her arm and kisses the inside of her wrist. They drive back along the highway.

Rita rides along, nearly unaware of her expanding elation until at the turnoff to their street she grasps Dean's forearm and laughs. "I'm all helium inside. I think I could float."

They round the corner. Something is going on in front of their unit. The light next to the front door burns bright as a flare. Charlie is outside, bare-chested, wearing a pair of ripped shorts. He has the large broom Rita brought years ago to sweep out the garage in the house where he was born. On the lawn, flowerpot shards lie like huge lost teeth. Charlie is pushing together a pile of red petals, black dirt, white roots, and leaves. He will swear to her that he doesn't know who did it, or why.

Dean kills the car's ignition at the curb, and he and Rita sit for a moment, watching Charlie. "I'm not just going to give him that money," Dean says. "He'll work for it. He's going to wax the car, clean the rain gutters. You'll see."

"It's not very much, is it," murmurs Rita. She strokes his arm. "Twenty-five dollars." She frowns at her son, repeating it to herself: twenty-five dollars. She can almost imagine finding it funny, someday.

THE
SKIRT

After this summer with Liss, I feel a certain surrender. I am open to the next part of my life. And so through these white-hot mornings I go, across the Mall behind government lawn-mowing squads, past late-season tourists browsing the snack carts for breakfast. I mount the marble steps to the great corniced box where I earn my pay. The security guard, who is dark browed and angry, watches me. I pause outside the glittering glass doors and lift my face to the heavens, in contemplation.

Are you an American taxpayer? I spend your money. I am an assistant grants assessor in the Department of Education. My name is Megan Rostow.

The summer truly began on June 19, the day of my murder fantasy. The air was wet and heavy in our lungs, brown blooms still clung to the azalea shrubs, and hazy

light hung from a thick roof of clouds. We drove, Barry
and Liss and I, out through the suburbs to the place where
the Potomac drops from the Appalachian plateau to begin
its mellow roll across the coastal plain. From parks along
the banks, from rocky outcrops shaded by trees or jutting
over the water, you can watch the river's great tumble.
Seven frolickers drown there each year. When we clambered up to the rock's high shoulder, Liss gasped at the
view, and sidled to the very edge of the granite. She gazed
at the white thunder of the rapids below us. I, however,
stared at the shorts she wore. Cuffed above the knee,
cotton, they were a butter-yellow, printed with curly
Venetian gondolas. They were my mother's; she'd fa-
vored clothes that told a story, sweaters with city maps
woven into them, dresses and slacks showing the signs' of
the zodiac or the makings of a garden salad.

Mom had been bottom-heavy, and I noticed now that
Liss, in her twentieth year, was beginning to take after
her. She stood looking across the river, toward a sky the
color of somebody's shaven underarm. Her wiry red curls
bent in the wet wind. "Those shorts are not flattering,"
I called to her over the water's tumult. She didn't hear
me. But Barry, propped next to me against a stove-warm
boulder, muttered, "Nice," as he opened a ragged
paperback on French legal history. He'd nestled a six-
pack of beer alongside himself, his legs outstretched and
his big bony feet freed from their tennis shoes. He was the
picture of a pleasant suburban outing. Liss sat down and
dangled her legs over the edge of the precipice, above the

racing river. I rested my head against the jagged wall at my back, shut my eyes, and pictured her disappearing beneath the snowy water. Without blood, without screams, she'd slip under the rapids and be gone.

The midday brightness soaked through my lids, and I felt a leadenness that made my calves and forearms ache. In the months following my mother's death, this great heaviness descended upon me for hours and days at a time. Since Liss's arrival the previous week, I'd felt engulfed. The river breeze riffling the pale hairs on the back of my neck seemed to mock my inert heart. I opened my eyes and rolled my head once more toward Liss. Her stretched-out tank top had come untucked in back, her shoulders were round and pinkening, her elbows rough. I imagined it again, nudging her over the edge. She'd vanish in a twinkling. Barry would run over—I'd push him, too, take the car, head for somewhere far and anonymous.

I shut my eyes again and felt a queasy chill pass through me. I put my hand on Barry's warm leg. The wind tangled in the lush trees beyond our backs. And the afternoon passed uneventfully, heavy with water roar and lukewarm beer. When we returned home, Liss discovered she'd been hired by Camp Victory for Teens at Risk.

We are the living remnants of the Rostows and the Hallorans, Melissa and I. There are cemeteries in the downy suburbs of Columbus where weather-resistant flowers deck the rest of them. Our surname is also everlasting back home, bolted in red steel script above an office-supply store, the still-thriving business my grandfather founded and my father took over until his death by drowning on a Jamaican holiday, 1974. My mother sold the store to the floor manager, Mr. Otis.

A tricky, lovely, wonderful woman, my mother was. And quick, bright—she should have been on television. She opened her own tax-preparation office instead. She never remarried, but it wasn't out of loyalty to my father; she searched, roaming the years with an open mind, but she never found anyone. The pain she must have felt, in that scrolled bed, night after night—for sixteen years! This thought knocks the wind from me. My mother's mother, Grandma Halloran, taught remedial reading right up until her death last year. Eight months after Grandma, last September, my mom was buried across town in the Rostow plot. The Rostows were a sprawling and attractive clan, but they lived in and around Leipzig, Germany, with a surplus of trust in the kindness of fate, or a puzzling lack of foresight. The exception was my grandfather David, who bolted across the Atlantic in '38 with his fat wife and small boy; the wife, Bella, and twin girls died in a lying-in hospital days after the U.S. entered the war.

Men of religion say death is a part of life, it's in the hands of God. I suppose I agree. But in the case of my mother, it seemed plain to me: the blame fell here, on earth.

.   .   .

When Liss found the summer job at Camp Victory, I was relieved. Not that I'd had time to worry about her; on my desk, proposals piled up: people wanting grants to track the learning curves of Cambodians or home schoolers or children who'd been driven by hunger to eat dirt and paint. I couldn't fret about my sister, and whether she had the presence of mind to change trains at the right stop, to steer clear of the shooting neighborhoods, to lock the street door behind her when she got to my place. I simply wanted her to be busy and out of my way until she returned to college in Columbus.

I'm sure it was illegal for the camp to give her a bus route. When she came home after her first day with the battered yellow van, I peered out the window at it. She dashed into the house, yelling, "You won't believe this."

"You can't drive kids around without a license for that," I said.

"The camp people tested me; they said just be careful till we get the chauffeur's license." She gathered her thick mop of hair in one hand and raised it off her neck, fanning herself with the other hand. "They think I can handle it." Her arms were rosy with sun. Down her loose sleeve I glimpsed a flesh-colored bra. Picking up an African violet from the windowsill, I pinched off some dead leaves. "You're hardly what I'd call responsible," I said, my chest tightening around my lungs. "Do these people know the first thing about you?" A flush rose in her face, her small bulbous nose. Her arms dropped to her sides and she stared at me a moment, eyes dark, lips slightly parted. I noticed she wore a thin gold chain of Grandma Halloran's. "You should probably mind your own business," she said, reaching for a light blue towel that was hanging from a corner of a bookcase. She'd brought her own linens from school. "I don't believe anybody requested your opinion." She turned and walked down the hall; then I heard the bathroom door shut and the old plumbing groan and knock as the shower sputtered to life. Cupping velvety rotted leaves in one hand, I paused by the closed door on my way to the kitchen garbage can. Her sobs rung hollowly against the shower's tiled walls.

The galaxy of siblings is ruled by ever-shifting forces, balances changing and orbs drifting in and out of each other's sphere of influence. For years, Liss was living out her dramas across vast reaches of space from me. She met with expensive tutors; she wailed in her sleep and sleepwalked into walls; she got caught at every forbidden thing she did. The week she shoved a girl down a flight of stairs and was suspended from the seventh grade, I won a scholarship to a girl's college in Virginia. She had never been my problem, I'd kept a clean distance from her messes, and once I left for school, she seldom occupied my thoughts.

But my mother's passing threw our planets out of whack. Early last December, I received a letter from her, from her freshman dorm.

My roommate asked if I wanted to come home to Barberton with her for Christmas break. Her dad was just fired so it might be strange. Also, she said we'd have to go to church.

My mother had converted before her marriage, but her faith waned after my father's death, and the holidays in our house passed aimlessly, without denomination. Liss, nine or ten years old, would beg to sleep over at a friend's house on Christmas Eve. Mom firmly refused: "They want to be with their own, and so should you."

Liss called me at work one morning soon after her letter arrived. "Your roommate sounds like fun," I said, striving for cheeriness.

"Really?" Her voice was brittle and so clear she could've been standing right there in my cubicle. "You really think so?"

"I made plans to go to a friend's ski condo," I said. "There could be room for you, but I don't know. . . ." When I hung up, my cheeks were hot with shame.

A week or so later the mail brought a ceramic incense burner with a postcard of a snowy Ohio scene tucked inside. "Happy Hanukkah/Christmas," it read. "Liss." I'll confess the use I found for the little perforated pot: holding Brillo pads beneath the kitchen sink. In return I sent a flowered scarf to Liss's dorm address, which was all I had. She wouldn't receive it until after New Year's.

. . .

When Liss's summer break rolled around, I didn't want to take her in. Barry said, "Megan, tell me something— where else can she go?" He and I met last Thanksgiving, at the feast of a colleague's family; he was the other stray. Though there was a difference between his orphanhood and mine: Barry's people (parents, aunts, step uncles, cousins) were simply far away, in Pacific Palisades. He had strange trifocal glasses and those large feet and hands. But right off the bat, I knew his shining qualities—kindness, patience—were things I could use in my life. Even so I suspected, in the guilty private depths of my grief, that soon I'd push off from him, as a rested swimmer leaves the lip of a pool.

"My heart goes out to her," he said to me one night in bed soon after Liss arrived. "She seems extremely forlorn." Then he kissed my stomach. In lovemaking, as in looks, he was awkward, I thought—but his energy and earnestness impressed me. On an evening in late June, Liss brought home a snapshot, and sitting next to her on the couch, Barry pored over it with interest. Besides chauffeuring the Northwest D.C. van pool, Liss was assistant counselor to a gang of twelve-year-olds, who'd posed for a group portrait standing on their heads. "What's this kid's name?" Barry said, pointing and scrutinizing. "She looks like she's thirty-five." His collar was unbuttoned, his tie undone; his glasses rode low on his thin nose. Leaning in the doorway, I tossed a stack of mail onto the coffee table.

"She's an incest victim, foster child. She can't read at

all.'' Liss looked up at me as I turned to leave the room. ''Remember that stuttering girl Dana in my sixth-grade class?'' she called after me.

''No,'' I said. In the bedroom now, I stripped off my skirt and my hose.

''This is the head counselor,'' I heard her say to Barry.

''Standing on his feet,'' he said. I pulled on cotton shorts, cherry-red, and a T-shirt. I walked back into the room and he said, ''New shorts.''

Liss set the picture facedown in her lap. ''You've got great legs,'' she said. I bent to shuffle through the mail. ''Mine are so sausagelike.'' She lifted a stubbly leg and extended it toward the coffee table, near my face.

''No, they're not,'' Barry said, with his unerring sense of what's required of him.

''Really?'' Her voice brightened. ''You think they're okay?''

''Sure, very sexy,'' said Barry.

''I don't know. My shins don't taper,'' said Liss, stretching the limb up into the air now, narrowly missing my nose.

''I'd say they're shapely,'' protested Barry.

This conversation was making me nauseated, in the way an extremely bad TV show sometimes will. I had to straighten up, walk to the kitchen, retrieve a crusted, sticky bottle of tomato juice from the refrigerator and pour myself a little, in order not to say something mean.

. . .

Some days later, on a dismal afternoon early in July, thunderclouds trolled the Mall with gray nets of rain. I emerged from work into the late afternoon, cringing beneath a ripped umbrella, and spied the van parked on the curb across the street, glowing brightly in the gloom like a gigantic canary melon. Liss cranked the window down and called to me. "We were passing by. I can give you a ride."

"I was going to stop at—" I gestured vaguely toward the shops down the block, but my feet in their low pumps were already soaked; around my ankles, my panty hose felt gummy. I splashed across the street and clambered into the passenger side, onto the moist vinyl. Liss had the driver's seat jacked up close to the wheel. A lone camper sat in the first bench behind us. Liss turned to him as she waited for a break in traffic. "Robert, this is my sister, Megan."

"Hey," he said, revealing silvery orthodontic wire. He was possibly fourteen years old, damp brown hair with long curls at the back of his neck, arrestingly large green eyes. On his T-shirt, the word LOPER was written in thick marker lines. He turned to stare out the window.

"Last on my route. He lives right over on Stanton Park." Liss struggled with the steering wheel, guiding the van's blunt nose through the rain-shimmering traffic. I couldn't recall being her passenger ever before. I turned back toward the boy. "Do your parents work on the Hill?" I instantly regretted this reference to his family—beatings and locked closets flashed luridly in my mind.

But he answered evenly. "My dad's a Senate aide. My mother lives in Texas." He turned his face up as we passed the Washington Monument, its top hidden in clouds.

"My group won the pizza this week," Liss said, wiping condensation from the windshield.

"They cheated," said Robert. "I bet you anything." At a small apartment block facing the weedy park, Liss pulled up to the curb. She shifted in her seat to watch Robert swing open the door. "See you tomorrow?"

"Yeah," he said, stepping down to the wet street. He was taller than I expected, crouching and waving shyly through the hatch. "See you." He slammed the door shut and dashed toward his building's broad awning, slinging a turquoise knapsack over his shoulder. His knees, poking out from khaki shorts, were knobby and tan. "He seems normal enough," I said.

"Well." Liss frowned, shifting gears, negotiating a tortured U-turn on the narrow street. "He tried to kill himself in April." Before us, green branches arched soaked and glittering above the street. Through the watery windshield, everything seemed coated with gel. She reached to fiddle with the vents. A blast of air lifted her bangs, exposing her milky forehead.

"Why? Anyone know?"

She shrugged. "Why not?"

I snorted at this. "You must be a wonderful influence," I said. But as the words left my mouth I was visited by a sudden flood of sorrow, over the gulf between us, over her wan desperation. Her mouth was working and her eyes bright as she maneuvered into a parking space across from my apartment. I checked the zippers on my briefcase. All around us and above us leaves bobbed and winked in the rain. "I can't get what your problem is," she whispered.

"Basically," I said, hugging the case to my chest, "I can't stand being around you." She nodded tightly at that, turned off the ignition, then yanked at the door handle and almost fell out of the van. Pushing the door shut behind her, she walked across the glistening street toward my building, bowing her head to the rain.

When I was Liss's age, I had a bad freshman year at college. I felt poorly prepared by our public high school, badly dressed. Mom would call me every day. "It'll take some time. You'll start to love it," she'd say. "I'm so proud of you." I'd picture her, coppery hair falling over the receiver in permanent waves, leaning against the kitchen counter, her lavender-and-black phases-of-the-moon pants smooth across her broad hips, her espadrilles, her gray eyes. I remember missing her terribly at those moments; I'd want to clutch her arms. Back then, I couldn't imagine my world without her.

During her freshman year, Liss took up poetry. She sent me a poem that arrived the day after Valentine's. I read the first lines

> I cross shining ice-filmed snow,
> the soundless howl of solitude—

and dropped the sheet of paper with a shudder: "Oh
God." Barry picked it up. "What's wrong?" He'd just
arrived with white roses; red ones had come the day
before. "I think she needs a boyfriend," I said, and
ripped the paper from the ivory blooms, arranging them
in a vase with the others. They looked waxen, I thought
as I stared at them. I knew that a bigger person than I
would have forgiven her more readily. A better sister
would have soothed her, shielded her from guilt. But
when I'd arrived in Columbus last September and
glimpsed Liss unkempt and alone in the airport, a word-
less, airless fury tented around me, expanding as the
reality of my mother's death—and the stupid truths sur-
rounding it—became plainer and plainer to me. I could
muster no sisterly compassion: none when I listened to
her blunder through a prayer at the interment, and none
when I left her five days later, on the opening morning of
fall semester, among the other newly arrived freshmen on
the front walk of a monolithic dormitory. She looked pale
and tragic, waving good-bye with her clothes in bulging
trash bags by her side. But what I felt as I watched her
was, I'm sorry to say, something close to disgust. Disgust
and rage. Because here is how it happened: Liss missed
her be-home-by-two-o'clock curfew; while clearing away
the dinner mess, my mother somehow brushed against
the oven dials and flipped open a gas jet. Then she lay
down in the adjoining den with a book. She could have
made it until the curfew easily, they say. They think she
could have made it until half past. But at three, Liss was

still searching for her lost car keys, having smoked much marijuana with a locker room attendant at the city pool. It was three-twenty when she found them. By then my mother, my rock and redeemer, was gone.

Gathering my umbrella and briefcase, I stepped out of the van and dodged black puddles up the front walk. Mom, Mom—she could almost be here. The circumstances that stole her from my life were, as you can see, so thin, so empty of significance—it made her achingly close to being alive.

The middle of July drifted past: dense sunshine dispersed by downpours, ragged men sprawled under the magnolia trees beside the Library of Congress. In the evenings and mornings, the air was filled with a limpid light that dulled the colors of the flowers and brought me close to tears as I walked back and forth from the Metro station with my suit jacket hanging over my arm. All the emotion of Liss's stay was beginning to wear me down. On July 2 3 I hit the office softball pool and won a weekend for two at Rehoboth Beach. Barry and I argued when I told him I was going alone. "I would like to know," he pleaded, his voice low in a restaurant, "why we are always proceeding on your terms—your terms." He leaned forward, clutching the sides of his plate as if it were nailed to the table. I gazed at my meat, miserable. "As if I should proceed on anyone else's," I said. "I can't see why I should."

The weather at the seashore was flawless, and from

my room on the high floor of a beachfront hotel the
crowds in their bright scraps looked like flowering
ground cover. Down on the boardwalk the smell of frying
fat mixed with the briny air, the cries of birds and children, music from radios, and the electronic burping and
honking of huge video arcades, all backed by the rumble
of the waves. I bought a lemon ice, spread my towel in
the boardwalk's shade, and sat with a book closed in my
lap, watching the brown-shouldered lifeguards signal one
another with flags, flinging a coded message from lofty
chair to lofty chair, above the heads of the crowd.
Soothed by the hiss and sizzle of retreating waves sliding
back into the sea, I watched the doings around me and
felt, finally, calm—more calm than I'd been in the eleven
months since Mom died. I scraped the last of the ice from
its waxy cup with the little wooden paddle and wondered
if I should perhaps slow things down with Barry, if we
should see less of each other. It was only fair. The idea
descended over me like silk; I knew I was right.

A giggling toddler, pursued by a pretty woman in a
modest outmoded bikini, stumbled across a corner of my
towel and tripped on my feet. Immediately, he erupted
in screams. The woman ran up and dropped to her knees,
panting lightly, and scooped him into her arms, cooing,
"Lukie, Lukie, don't cry," brushing sand first from his
blubbery legs and then from my towel. She smiled up at
me apologetically, laugh lines around her blue eyes. "He
must be a handful," I said.

"Oh, no, he's an angel." She stood up and cradled his

head against her shoulder. "Aren't you, sweetie?" He'd stopped crying; pressing his cheek to her tan body, he looked at me with round eyes. "I'll get you a bomb pop," the woman crooned, carrying him off past blankets and blow-up water floats and striped umbrellas.

I thought of Liss, alone in my place back in the city. Most likely, she did not remember our two family visits to the shore in Maine. She would have been no older than that little boy. I vaguely recalled her spitting up as we ate sandwiches in a touring launch. She might assume she'd never seen the ocean. My mother and I had both avoided reminiscing about such times spent with my father; I suppose we feared it would be too painful. But now, burying my wooden spoon in the sand, I suspected we'd simply hoarded those memories, my mom and I, guarding them jealously like tattered notes to be read in secret. When Liss used to knock on my bedroom door and ask me, was his hair red-brown like hers or red-orange, did he read all those books in the basement, I'd say, why're you asking me, I can't remember. And Mom would give only the vaguest answers and say, he loved you very much, Liss, and you will always know that. At some point in her pubescence Liss quit asking about him, but by her bed she kept a dim gray baby portrait, made in Germany.

I ended the weekend refreshed and relaxed, and not even the traffic crawling through fumes from Kent Narrows to the far side of the Bay Bridge deflated my mood. Cutting across the city through the Sunday-evening streets, I noticed how, even in the saddest neighborhood near the football stadium, families smiled down at smoking barbecue grills, teen couples walked hand in hand, and trees shaded the streets with a dusky summer beauty.

As I turned the key in my front-door dead bolt I made a silent oath, that I'd try to inject a new tone into my dealings with my sister. I flung the door open and dropped my bag in the entry. "Liss? Hi!"

I heard a hinge whine, and peering down the dark hallway, I saw the door of my bedroom slowly closing, as if under its own power. "Hi," Liss said from behind it. "I'm—I'll be right out, one sec." A pause. "How was the beach?" There was a strange quaver to her voice—she could have been jogging in place, or hopping.

"Crowded but nice." My old swim-team windbreaker lay on the floor; I picked it up and hung it in the closet. "What're you doing in there?"

"I'm changing." I heard her moving behind the door as I shouldered my bag again and passed through the hall toward the kitchen, where the laundry machines were tucked in a closet. My sandy clothes would go directly into the wash; I always unpack within moments of returning from a trip. I turned the dial and sent hot water streaming loudly into the washer, then went to the refrigerator. Staring into this largely empty vault, I heard, over the water's rush, a faint thud. I straightened and glanced out the window. Through the blue evening murk, I saw the camper Robert hurrying across the overgrown back plot, a T-shirt slung around his neck and a sneaker clutched in either hand. Pushing open the rusting gate, he began to run down the alley, barefoot, broken glass and all.

With a violent clunk, the washing machine swung into its agitation cycle. I crossed to it, and dropping the clothes into its maw piece by piece, staring as they were sucked into the vortex, I struggled to calm my quickening pulse, to get my spiraling anger under control. Please, I said to myself, please. I sprinkled powder straight from the box, without measuring, and went to sit down in the darkening front room, clinging to the sofa cushions with both hands. In a few moments, Liss dawdled in, her hair in a messy knot atop her head. "How about getting Chinese food for dinner?" she suggested timidly.

"You do what you want." I thought about going to bed, to sleep, oblivion—but then an image of my daisy-festooned sheets, and of Liss and the boy tangled in them, passed sickeningly before my eyes. "I'm going to Barry's," I said.

He received me gladly, poured me a beer, and allowed me my silence; I sat all evening slumped in an easy chair in his small study, watching him read, feeling my resolve to change things between us dissipating in the lamplight like vapor.

At work the next day I was distracted from a major project—the dispensing of tens of millions to teachers of creationism—by the thought of my sister luring a suicidal youth into her delinquent clutches. I had to stay late to get my tasks completed. The street was empty and full of shadows when I finally turned on to my block. I passed

the van, parked in a dark gap between streetlamps; something moving within it caught my eye. Cautiously, main-
taining a distance of several feet, I peered inside. I saw a
pair of thin shoulder blades, and a slowly waving foot,
white and smooth as cheese. And what was that glistening
object atop the headrest? The boy's retainer. Backing
away, I stumbled toward my door. Once inside, I triple-
locked it, and even engaged the little chain, my head
buzzing. In the kitchen, I pulled the phone book from
above the refrigerator and found the listing: "Loper,
Blake," on Fourth Street, Northeast. I dialed the number. A recorded voice answered, a man both businesslike
and bashful. At the tone I hesitated and hung up.

In the back window was a reflection of the kitchen,
with its fluorescent striplight over the sink. I stepped into
the picture. My navy skirt flickered a mysterious plum
purple in the reflection, and I saw I'd gone all day with
my blouse buttoned wrong. My eyes were hidden by light
bouncing off my glasses. I heard a key rattling in the
front-door lock. It stopped, then started again, a skittery,
trapped little thing, trying and failing, trying and failing,
to turn the bolt. Then came a sharp yelp from the buzzer
followed by a knock on the heavy door. I stared at my
image in the kitchen window. Where would she go? I
imagined the leering sidewalk drinkers over by the
Chicken Stop. And then I thought of the skinny boy, with
his bony knees. And of my mother's body curled on the
plaid daybed in the den.

In the living room, lit by the misty orange glow of the

anticrime streetlamps, I found Liss's vinyl suitcase stuffed under the TV table. Her belongings were heaped in a corner of the room, behind a stereo speaker, where the carpet succumbed to mildew every spring. The damp smell lingered there and mingled with the scent of Liss's clothes—a faint mixture of summer sweat and baby powder. Snatching a jersey from the top of the pile, I pushed it into the bag, then a pair of cutoff shorts and a tiny hardcover copy of *100 Love Poems.* I grabbed another handful from behind the speaker and yanked out a bundle of thinner cotton garments. Even in the half-light, I instantly recognized my mother's things—not just the gondola shorts were there, but the phases-of-the-moon pants, a panda-bear-and-bamboo sleeveless top, and a skirt that cradled in its folds memories of such intensity that I held its fine weave to my face and burst into tears, squatting there in the corner of my living room floor. The skirt was a silken swirl she'd worn to milestone events in the 1970s, piano recitals, grade school graduations, an eighth-grade dance she'd chaperoned; and I remembered her dressed in it, heading out with my father on a Saturday night; I watched from the front step as he opened the car door for her and waved good-night to me. Its pearl-gray crêpe was sprinkled with black-and-emerald sketches: from lutes to electric, it showed the whole history of guitars, and when she wore it I secretly shivered with pride at having a mother who was both with-it and demure.

Shattering glass interrupted my bawling; I looked up,

through tears, at flying shards. Jerking away, I landed hard on my rump, my left hand coming down on sharp fragments. I cursed and brought the hand to my lap, peering up at the window. A wicked-looking hole, framed by glinting points, gaped in the lower pane. Liss's face, wide-eyed and aghast, shone white in the void. "For Christ's sake," I spat, "what're you doing?" She winced, holding the treacherous bulk of a holly shrub away from her face with one hand. "I was locked out," she said. She lifted her other hand and showed me a tire iron.

Sighing, I turned the locks and swung the front door open for her, and in the glare of the stoop light, I saw that I'd stanched the bleeding with the sacred skirt, and that I'd bled quite a lot. A large brick-red blotch stained the material just below the back of the waistband. As Liss emerged from the bushes with the tire iron in one hand and scratches on her bare legs, she said, "You were here?"

I waved the skirt. "Who gave you these clothes?"

"Ma gave them to me."

I stepped inside and Liss followed, shutting the door behind her. I crossed the living room to the pile of clothes and kicked it softly. "All her favorites?"

"Last summer, she decided she wanted to wear only solids. Beige and black." With the edge of her sneaker, Liss started rounding up the larger slices of window glass. She looked up at me. "She went to a color consultant, and they told her that: black and beige." Something about the intimate way she gazed at me reminded me that my eyes and nose must have been red, tear-splotched. I held up my bloody palm and the skirt. "Look."

In the bathroom, I patted some toilet paper onto my palm and wrapped an Ace bandage around it. I heard Liss getting the broom from the hall closet, and the small noises of the glass being swept up. Slipping into my dark bedroom, I sat on the unmade bed, my stiff bandaged hand resting next to my leg like a dead crab. "I'm sorry," I called. The broom's rustle stopped, and she yelled, "Okay." A few ringing seconds of silence, then the sweeping started again. My arms and legs felt limp and loose. I thought about my mother in beige and black, and it didn't seem right, not at all. But what do I know, I thought, staring hollow-hearted out the window at weeds swaying in the dark garden heat.

There are certain episodes of sexual misbehavior in the Rostow and Halloran histories. My uncle Ted, Mom's only brother and a patriot who died on a peacetime mission in the Suez Canal, enlisted in the army after being fingered for a schoolmate's pregnancy. Grandma Halloran, perhaps to deflect attention from her son's transgression, told us shortly before she died that in 1949, a student had come to her in tears, distraught that her boss at Rostow's—old Opa himself—had offered her a hundred dollars for a hug—and she'd accepted it. "I told her to give the money to charity," Grandma said. And then there's my mother and the junior-high vice principal, Leff, witnessed passionately kissing in a downtown park-

ing lot by a large group from Liss's ninth-grade class, who
were waiting for a car pool home from dancing school.
Needless to say, this brought Liss in for a good deal of
ridicule. And worse, it was clear that Mom did not even
like Leff so very much.

Liss comported herself admirably, putting a stop to
her liaison. She couldn't bring herself to meet with Mr.
Loper face-to-face, but she did speak with him at length
on the phone, and it was finally agreed that if she gave up
the Camp Victory job and promised never to contact the
boy, no charges would be pressed.

That I could grant Liss a measure of my admiration
only after the perpetration of two felonies (statutory rape
is punishable by prison in every state and—Barry assured
us—the application of tire iron to windowpane is forced
entry even between sisters) is a fact of which I am not at
all proud. I certainly wish it could have come about some
better way. The plight of poor Robert is something that
will needle me until I hear he's well settled in a good job
or marriage—and even after that I'll worry.

The day after Liss was dishonorably discharged from
Camp Victory, on the first of August, a file-clerk slot
happened to open up in the library of Barry's firm, and
he offered to see what he could do. But Liss decided, and
I did not disagree, that it might be best for her to return
to Columbus and find a cheap student sublet for the rest
of the summer. "They're easy to get," she said, "and
you can rent them by the week." She took a tour of the
Capitol Building her last morning in town, and it was

raining when we took her to the airport that afternoon, with an unsettling green tint sifting down the western sky. Barry drove a new Japanese car he'd recently bought, and I sat beside him, with Liss in back. As we passed the Pentagon and its murky, moatlike lagoon, Liss leaned forward and said that she'd left me the skirt with the guitars. "I thought you could fit into it better. That thing only fit Mom in her skinnier days."

"There's a big bloodstain on the back," I said.

"You can get it out with bleach." An arriving plane pressed down through the air above us and shot over the airport fence.

"Then it'll have a bleach stain on it."

"That's better than blood—right?" she said, and slid back on the seat. The rain spattered against the windows. She sighed. "Not a good day to fly."

"Actually," said Barry, glancing up at the sky, "pilots become more alert in bad weather."

We found a place in a pay lot, then crowded under my umbrella, threading toward the terminal between cars and oily puddles. Barry's remark still filled my ears, chiming there, words rolling; and now, days later, I am still hearing it. There is something so deeply comforting about that remark, I think—something so loving, so noble, so entirely good. When I watched him lift Liss's bag onto a passing redcap's cart, his dark head bowed as he heaved the load up, I decided that a man who can think of such a thing to say is a man to be cherished, to be treasured. I furled the dripping umbrella, and actually contemplated a life with him. Glass doors slid open, and I followed Barry, Liss, and the redcap into the building, hurrying dutifully behind as they snaked through the crowds, flushing businessmen from their path, dodging children.

A BOUT
THE
AUTHOR

Debra Jo Immergut was born in Columbus, Ohio, and grew up in Rockville and Potomac, Maryland. She currently lives in Berlin.